SPELL BREAKER

LEGENDS OF THE FALLEN BOOK 2

J.A. CULICAN

H.M. GOODEN

ISBN-13: 978-1-949621-06-8

ISBN-10: 1-949621-06-5

Dragon Realm Press

www.dragonrealmpress.com

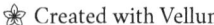 Created with Vellum

For all our readers who lost themselves in the world of Lynia.

CONTENTS

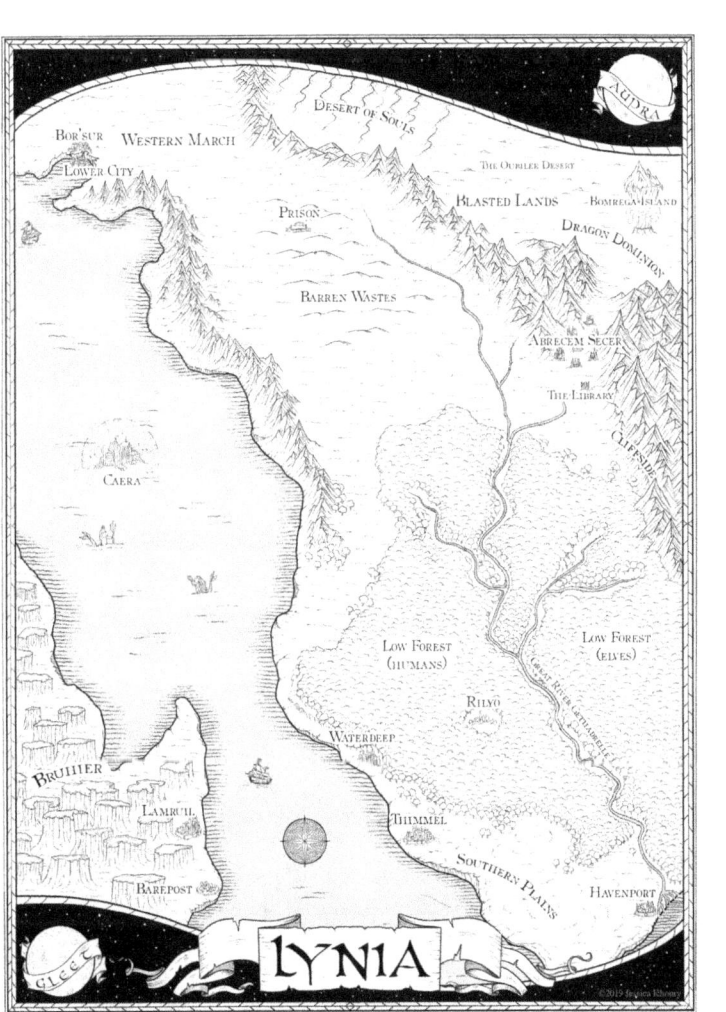

AUDRA

Desert of Souls

Bor'sur   Western March
Lower City

The Ourbler Desert

Prison   Blasted Lands   Boirega Island
                                              Dragon Dominion

Barren Wastes

                                              Abrecem Secer

                                              The Library
                                                            Cliffside

Caera

                                    Low Forest   Low Forest
                                    (Humans)   (Elves)

                                    Rilyo

                        Waterdeep

Bruhier
                                    Thimmel
        Lamruil
                                              Southern Plains
        Barepost   Havenport

GLEET

LYNIA

CHAPTER 1

"I'll find you."

Dag'draath's chilling voice echoed through the hallway, barely audible over the sound of my heels clicking on the concrete prison floor as I ran, turning my head to see if he was behind me.

No one was there.

A small grey door appeared to my left. Quickly, I tried the handle, heart leaping as it turned. Darting in, I sought refuge on the other side, and closed the door. Leaning on it briefly, my hand over my heart, I willed it to slow as my eyes closed. Meticulously I breathed rhythmically to the count of three, grateful when the beat eased to a more manageable speed.

I was in control of my body again.

Turning slightly, I placed my ear against the door and strained to hear what was happening on the other side. Silence greeted my efforts. Barely breathing, I waited until I was certain I was alone. My eyes swept over the dark room. The only light I could discern came through a large crack in the wall, perhaps created during a prison revolt. In any event, I was happy to have it.

Moving away from the darkness, I paced back and forth, turning my head from side to side until I became familiar with the room and its contents. Dust covered every surface, as if I was the first person to be here in years. I ran my finger along the top of a table, stopping when my shin connected with a wooden box below. I knelt and slid it out.

I took a moment to examine it, still uncertain about my safety, but anxious for any possible clues. It was about two feet in size, composed of a dark wood which was difficult to make out in the dim light. I lifted its top. The darkness made it impossible to see what was inside, so I reached in.

My fingers brushed something cold and round. I flinched reflexively before I extended them again. It was too heavy to lift with one hand, but I was already committed. Adding the other hand, I reached beneath the object and lifted.

The scant light bounced off a glass ball, reflecting around to illuminate more of the room. The place had clearly been deserted for a long time and I shuddered.

I placed the ball on top of another box close to the hole in the wall, placing it objectively for use as a light source to explore the room more fully. Grabbing a cloth, I had spotted draped over a nearby chair, I stuffed it into the crack at the bottom of the door to keep light from escaping and potentially giving away my location.

On the right side of the room stood a large cabinet with its door blocked by a large rock and various other objects near the base. As quietly as possible, I removed the smaller items around the rock. There was a reason this cabinet had been secured, and I wanted to find out. I leaned over, trying to slide the rock across the floor since it was far too large to lift.

I pushed with everything I had, but it didn't budge. Why hadn't I been blessed magic? Or even muscles? I gritted my teeth, placing one foot on the rock and my back against the wall, and grunted as I tried to use the wall to my advantage.

To my surprise, the rock moved an inch, maybe two. I got back into position and tried again. This time the rock moved enough to give me enough space to open the door wide enough to peek at the contents inside the cabinet.

I lifted the latch and the door came free. I pushed it open until it couldn't go any farther due to the rock, but now the door blocked the ball's light. The interior was a yawning pit of darkness.

Squirming a little, I gathered the courage to reach my hand inside. "Don't be ridiculous. Nothing inside will hurt you. You just did the same thing with the box and it was totally fine."

I let out a deep breath, leaning forward, and I stuck my arm past the edge of the door into the abyss of the cabinet.

At first, I felt nothing.

I advanced my fingers, groping for something I could pull out. "Ouch."

I yanked my hand back. Blood dripped to the floor, falling from a deep cut my index finger from whatever it had touched.

Using the thumb and forefinger from my good hand to apply pressure, I managed to use my other fingers to release the pouch hanging from my waist. I shook the contents over the cut and used the heat from my hand to form a seal over the injury.

I'd been practicing since freeing Beru. I wouldn't take the chance of becoming injured and being unable to heal myself while I dreamwalked again.

The rock was going to have to move farther to allow light inside the cupboard. I hoisted myself against the wall and shoved the rock a good foot—in the wrong direction. I swung my head back, cracking it hard on the wall.

I needed a new plan.

I moved to the other side of the cabinet, placed my hands on the floor, pressed my back against the wall and pushed. It moved—in the right direction. I pushed again and the door was free.

Jumping to my feet I placed my hand on the edge and hesitated. My nerves revved and I forced them back down.

I swung the door open.

"Aria, it's time to get up. It's awkward trying to entertain Beru without you." Gavin's voice boomed as he entered my bedroom.

I shot up in my bed, disoriented by the daylight streaming onto the bed. I blinked slowly, and as my surroundings came into clearer focus, I realized I was home, in my bedroom on my parent's farm.

"Were you dreamwalking?" Gavin wheeled himself over to my bed.

"Yes."

"Did you find it?"

"No, but I think I'm getting close."

I sat up and swung my legs over the side of my bed, letting the warmth of the bright sun cover me. I closed my eyes and bathed in it momentarily.

"Get dressed. Food is on the table." He turned and wheeled himself out of my room.

I stood up, stretched my arms, and cracked my neck. It was good to be home. To see Damour and Vinsha, their baby, Brock, and my parents. Most of all, I'd succeeded in keeping my promise to Damour—I'd brought Gavin home.

I slipped into comfortable clothes, intending to work the fields with Father after breakfast. Arriving in the great room, I watched Damour scramble eggs as Vinsha bounced Brock on her knee and Mother rubbed his back. Father sat at the table, already eating with Gavin. My eyes swept the room, searching for the other person who should be at the table.

"He's outside." Father pointed toward the door with his fork, then returned to his meal.

Smiling, I practically bounced toward the door, unable to hide my pleasure at being home again. I'd dreamt about this moment for many moons. I swung the door open and stepped outside, gazing joyfully at my childhood home.

Beru sat by the firepit with his head low, his ghostly pale skin now slightly burnt from the suns it hadn't seen for centuries.

"Did you eat?"

"Yes, thank you. Your family has been gracious to me."

"You're welcome here. Always."

Beru glanced up long enough for our eyes to meet. His dark brown eyes were rimmed red and when he blinked and looked away.

I knew he'd been crying.

He poked at the fire, adding brush to avoid further eye contact. "Did you dreamwalk?"

"Yes. I didn't find anything yet." I moved close enough to toss a handful of brush into the fire. "Father have you on brush duty?"

"I offered." The corners of his lips turned up in a half smile, his eyes darting toward me, then back down.

Poor Beru.

Father had kept him busy with work since the moment we'd stepped foot on the farm. *Idle hands equal wickedness,* he always said. My family wasn't happy I'd brought him here. It had taken much discussion before they'd reluctantly agreed he could stay —for now.

"I know you'd rather be anywhere but here. To finally be out prison just to be stuck on a farm—"

"I like it just fine." He reached out, placing his hand on my arm.

For a moment I could only blink at the sight of his callused hand against my arm, surprised he'd touched me to respond. I cleared my throat and smiled nervously as I pulled away, gesturing to the house.

"Okay. I'm going back in for some grub. Care to join me for seconds?"

"I'm fine right here. Go be with your family."

I nodded, swallowing back a lump in my throat.

He may finally be out of prison, but he had nothing to go back home for.

I'd walked all the way to the house before I glanced back and caught him staring.

He'd been watching me leave.

I gave him a wave and continued to the house, wondering what he was thinking.

"Your plate is getting cold," Damour chided as I stepped into the dining room.

I smiled my thanks as I slipped into my seat, attacking the food in front of me. I still hadn't become reaccustomed to hot food and didn't think I'd stop being amazed by how much better it tasted than cold meat and bread on the trail.

"I ate your ham." Gavin wheeled out of my reach when I threatened him with a swat.

"There's more." Damour placed a large plate of ham in the middle of the table, shaking his head at Gavin's mischievous expression.

"I'm off to the fields. I'll take that one with me." My father pointed his chin to the door.

I'd noticed he seemed to be trying to separate Beru from me as much as he could. I hadn't mentioned it and wondered if he had noticed as well.

"You be nice to that boy," Mother scolded him as she helped into his work overcoat.

He scoffed. "He's no boy."

"You hold your tongue with him," she called out as he left.

He slammed the door, the rusted hinges groaning in objection of the treatment.

"Wonder what that's all about?" Damour winked.

"What do you mean?" I sat straighter, unsure if I wanted him to reply or not.

"Enough. None of us know what it's been like for him. Until he shows us disrespect, you will all treat him with kindness." She gave us a warning look before sitting back down at the table and reaching for a piece of ham.

"He's taken to Brock," Vinsha interjected softly, placing the baby on the floor.

Brock crawled over to Mother and she picked him up, cooing down at her pride and joy. He was never on the floor long with her around, much to Vinsha's dismay.

"He needs to crawl, Mother." She took Brock and placed him back on the floor—farther from his grandmother this time.

"He'll catch a cold from that dirty floor."

"Mother." Damour turned from the stove, his eyebrows furrowed slightly.

"I can tell I'm not needed here." She stomped across the room and shoved her feet into her boots. "I'll be in the fields."

"Mother." Damour called after her as the door slammed again.

"What's with her?" I placed my fork on the empty plate which he filled with more eggs before I could protest.

"She's called Brock 'Harov' a couple times." He sat across from me, a sad look on his face as he loaded his plate with ham.

"Really?"

"Yeah." He jammed a large piece of ham in his mouth.

"Do you think it's what Grandpa had?"

He jammed more meat in his mouth as he looked toward me, his narrowed eyes and full mouth clear indicators he didn't want to have this conversation.

"I'm going to put him down," Vinsha picked Brock up and snuggled him as she crooned a tune, leaving the room.

"What are you going to do with him?"

"Beru?" I turned to Damour, surprised.

"Have you brought anyone else home?"

I raised an eyebrow at his broad sarcasm. "Not yet."

"Seriously, how long is he going to be staying?"

"I'm not sure. I need him in case..." I stopped myself before I said what everyone was thinking.

"Until the others all leave."

"They don't know about the tear. No one is looking yet."

"They know he left? That he's not hiding somewhere?" He filled his plate with another round of eggs and ham, looking at me sideways.

"Yes." I finished the last bite of food on my plate, chewing slowly as I avoided his gaze.

He blamed me as the others did. They didn't understand why I couldn't leave him there or send him back in once I freed him.

"It'll all work out."

"You think so?"

"Sure. They haven't gotten out. The longer it is, the less likely they will look for a way out."

"I'm not upset with what I did, but I'm afraid of what could happen if..." I put my hands in my lap, uncertain he would understand what I meant without having seen what the prison was like.

"You mustn't worry until something happens. They have no reason to believe they could also be freed. It will work out." He stood and took our plates to the sink.

"So, what do I do with Beru until then?" I got up from the table and walked over to help with the dishes.

"Don't worry. Father will work him to death." He laughed as he clanked the dishes in the sink.

I threw a towel toward him, lifting myself onto the counter as I looked at him. "I'm serious."

"It's not up to you. He has to choose what he wants to do.

Anyone with eyes can see he feels duty-bound to you for freeing him." He placed a pot of water on the stove to boil.

I watched his efficient movements absently as I swung my legs back and forth. "He has no duty to me."

"So why hasn't he left already?"

I glanced toward the window. If I had to guess, it was because he had nowhere else to go. No matter what my brother thought, I knew I needed him more than he needed me. One day, Dag'draath would find the tear, and he and all his most depraved soldiers would be freed from prison.

And it would be all my fault.

CHAPTER 2

"One, two, three..."

I often counted when anxiety overcame me. Yes, even warriors get anxious. When you're about to knock on the door of the woman who threw you out of her home the last time you saw her, it's wise to be nervous.

Especially when that woman was Mother Ofburg.

Sleep had been elusive the night before, as the many ways my visit could go danced through my head. Maybe time had healed her anger, and she wouldn't slam the door in my face the second she saw me.

But when I stepped up on her front stoop, the door swung open before I could knock, and my hand dropped.

From the look on her face, it was clear time had *not* healed all. "What are you doing here?" She swept dust directly into my face.

"I need to talk to you." I stepped back, coughing as the dust hit the back of my throat.

"Nothing you can say will change my opinion of you."

Her stout frame blocked the entrance into the house, and she brandished her broom like a staff in front of her, blocking me from pushing past into the house, not that I was crazy enough to even consider it.

"Please." I hated to beg, but I needed her guidance to help me get back to my normal life. I wanted to be a healer. I needed to. After what I'd seen, healers were going to be needed more than ever.

"I have no time for deceit." She slammed the door shut, the harsh click of a lock sliding into place emphasizing her words.

"I'll talk through the door," I waited for a response.

Nothing.

I raised my voice and tried again. "Loud enough for the neighbors to hear."

The door swung open. She stood with her broom firm in her hand, glowering at me, nostrils flaring with anger. Then to my surprise, stepped back.

I took her cue and walked into the kitchen, sitting at the table while I waited for her to say something.

She closed the door, and for a moment, just stood there as if trying to decide what to do about me. "You have until my cake is done. I don't expect it will be terribly long."

She placed her broom against the wall and sat opposite me, crossing her arms as she looked coolly down her nose at me. She wore lines I didn't remember, and guilt poured through me at the thought of what she'd lost because of me.

"Thank you for hearing me out."

"I have no choice, apparently." She took a long sip from her glass, looking away from me.

"I'm sorry for everything that's happened. It's all my fault, but I never asked for any of it. I never asked to be a dreamwalker. I never asked to be the person to free Beru." How could I reason away her pain? It was all true, but I knew it wouldn't help.

"You freed a monster." She slammed her hands on the table as she glared at me, half-standing from her chair.

"There's so much you don't know." I leaned closer, pleading with her, yearning to see the old Mother Ofburg. Even a small glimpse would mean so much.

"There's nothing you can tell me that will change my mind. All of a sudden, you can dreamwalk and know everything? Oh, and if that isn't just like you."

"I don't know everything, but I know Beru. He's not what people say of him." I pushed away from the table and paced the room, raking my fingers through my hair. I needed her to trust me again, but could she?

Mother Ofburg rose the rest of the way and stormed over to the fire, lifting the top off the pot suspended there. "It's done."

"I've barely spoken."

"That's all the time I have. I've heard enough." She turned to the cake, removing it from the fire.

"I want to come back. I want to be a healer again." I watched as her movements slowed.

"You were never a healer. And now you're a dreamwalker."

For the first time since I returned, she sounded like the Mother Ofburg of old briefly.

"I want to be a healer and learn from you. I promise to take it more seriously. I'll study and be present. I won't fool around. I promise."

I stood at attention and prayed for her to accept me again.

"Your time here would be wasted as a healer. You must practice dreamwalking. It's too dangerous not to take seriously."

The hint of concern in her voice was obvious and unexpected, but it wasn't enough. Though I tried not to, I still longed for her approval.

"Couldn't we try? You mentioned training me to dreamwalk." I clasped my hands together, realizing with a vague sense of surprise they were trembling.

"Most of my assistants are dead. So, no. I don't need another child to look after. It was a favor to your parents, that's all. I owe them nothing now." She turned back to the fire, showing me a stiff back as she stoked the coals until they burned bright orange.

The fire seemed to be mocking the pain burning in my chest. "It was just a favor to my parents?" Blinking several times, I willed away my tears, steadying myself with a hand on the chair as the room spun slowly around me.

"Yes, that was all. A favor." She kept her back to me, tending the fire as if it was the most important thing to her.

Blood rushed to my face as anger mixed with embarrassment and pain. I turned away from her to flee, knocking over my chair as tears blurred my vision. Ignoring it, I ran out the door and didn't stop until after I'd passed a tear-misted version of her gate.

Had the past few years studying healing under her tutelage only happened at the request of my parents? I pushed the thought away, trying to process it. Surely, she'd meant they'd inquired about her assistance.

I meandered through the village. I needed time to think before returning home. I hadn't dared wonder what the future held when I'd left here, save for my mission to bring Gavin home. I'd always assumed I'd go back to being a healer again, and my life would be the same as before. How foolish I'd been.

Wiping residual tears from my cheeks, I dragged my feet along the road filled with the familiar yet new. Most of the buildings had been rebuilt or were in the process of after the ur'gel attack had destroyed so much of the town.

"Traitor," a woman spat at my feet as she passed me.

I stopped, turning to look at her with confusion. Had she been speaking to me? No, that was ridiculous. I shook my head, sighing, and continued, clasping my hands behind my back and keeping my head down as I watched my plodding feet on the dirt lift small clouds of dirt.

I was almost to the cobbler's shop when the owner exited

the door with a bucket of waste and dumped the contents on the street merely a foot from me. A drop of the foul-smelling water splashed on my shoe.

I jumped back in disgust. "Hey, watch where you're throwing that!"

He marched back into his shop, slamming the door behind him but not before I caught his reply. "I missed."

Did he mean to say he'd meant to hit me?

I shook my head to clear the paranoid thought.

He'd always been pleasant in the past. Maybe he was having a bad day.

But as I continued walking, I began to take note of the strange way people were acting.

They avoided eye contact or wrinkled their noses as I passed, as if I disgusted them.

One woman even pulled her child away protectively as she passed me, walking faster, and glancing back with a mixture of fear and disgust.

Unable to believe what I was seeing, I veered away from the street and took a shortcut through an alley to avoid the main road, picking up my stride until I was running as fast as I could toward the woods.

I slowed when my breath caught in my chest and I was far enough away from town I was sure no one was watching. How could this be happening?

My neighbors seemed to hate me and had either shunned or expressed their hatred outwardly. Surely, they would have done the same to save their families.

How could they be judging me so harshly?

A hand tugged my arm back and I swung around, grabbing my knife with my free hand.

"Whoa!" Sade stood behind me, holding her hands up as she stepped back.

"Sorry, I didn't hear you." I placed my knife back in its

sheath.

"Were you crying?"

"No."

"What's going on?"

"Oh, nothing. Just everyone hates me apparently."

"Everyone?"

"Pretty much." I inhaled raggedly as a tiny sob escaped from my lips.

"So, you were in the village then." She bobbed her head, walking past me, before turning to give me what appeared to be a sympathetic look.

"You knew?" My face burned at the thought of Sade having kept this from me.

Had she enjoyed my downfall? From the well-liked healer's apprentice to the town pariah?

"You didn't?" She stopped, turning to me with raised eyebrows. "What did you think? They would all embrace you for freeing Beru?"

"No. But I didn't think I'd almost be drenched in urine." I held my hands out, unsure if any of the liquid had fallen anywhere aside from my shoe.

"Urine?" She barked with laughter, before muffling the rest of her amusement with a hand when I glared.

"Don't you dare laugh at me."

She continued chuckling despite my threat and ran away from me.

I gave chase, and soon we were both laughing and running between the trees like fools.

"Okay. I give up." She held her stomach as she leaned over and tried to catch her breath.

I rested on a tree. While it certainly wasn't funny, I knew Sade was on my side and the lighthearted teasing had gone a long way toward soothing my wounded pride.

"I went to see Mother Ofburg."

"How'd that go?"

I paused, not ready to relive the painful moment so soon, finally settling on the reason I'd gone to her house in the first place. "She won't mentor me."

"And you're surprised?"

I didn't bother answering, choosing to stomp on the ground as we walked. It may be immature, but it made me feel less angry.

"This is why I prefer to be alone. Humans *suck*."

"Maybe you're on to something." I certainly wouldn't feel so hurt with less human interaction. Perhaps, just for the next little while, until things blew over. Whenever that was.

"I have something to cheer you up," she shot me a mischievous grin. "Come on." She took off through the forest.

I did my best to catch up but keeping her in sight was all I could manage.

When she finally stopped, it was in the center of the clearing near the miller's field. The sun shone brightly now it was unencumbered by the branches of the trees. "Your surprise." She gestured for me to go ahead.

"An empty field?" I raised an eyebrow, perplexed, but walked past. I'd had enough surprises to last me a lifetime the past few months, and wasn't excited about one more.

"You don't see it?" She ran past me into the middle of the field. "Are you *scared*?"

I rolled my eyes at her childish glee and ran to catch up. As the top of the grain touched my fingertips as I ran, thoughts of my childhood rushed back. I missed the days when life had been so innocent and a hard day of working on the farm in the hot sun was the worst thing to happen to me.

"Now can you see it?" She stopped, turning toward a mountain of hay.

My heart leapt. "Astor and Iri!" I ran to them.

Iri scooped me up in his strong arms.

I yelped as he spun me around, almost crushing me and when he let me go, I dropped to the ground and turned to Astor for a gentler hug.

"What are you doing here?" I stepped back, holding him at arm's length.

"I'm here to protect him from himself." Iri pointed toward Astor, a patent falsely aggrieved look on his face.

"More like I've come with a message, and this big lug offered to take me."

Astor slapped Iri on the chest in reply and he grunted, folding his arms.

"A message? For whom?" Curiosity plagued me. I hadn't expected to see them so soon. Or, perhaps ever, to be honest.

"For you." Astor stepped closer, reaching for my hands with a solemn expression.

"Why do you have a message for me?" I pulled away, uncertain I liked the reason they were visiting.

"There's a new dreamwalker in Western March. She wishes to speak to you." The smile on Astor's face seemed strained.

I tried my best to read him but came up empty. "And if I don't want to speak to this dreamwalker?"

"Why wouldn't you want to?" He wrinkled his forehead. This time it was easy to read his confused look.

"I'm done with all of that." I walked past, brushing him off with a wave of my hand as I tried to hide my frustration at the turn of events. Why couldn't things just go back to normal?

"She wants a dream meeting."

I heard his footsteps behind me. Shaking my head, I strode away. "I'm busy with the farm."

"Oh, come on. You're no farm girl!" He called after me.

I turned to face him, embarrassed by how I was treating him. It wasn't his fault a dreamwalker wanted to meet with me.

"Here, take this." He walked up to me, gently placing a small stone in my hand.

"What is it?" I accepted out of curiosity, flipping it over to get a better look. It was red and beautifully polished, with little flecks of gold that sparkled in the sunlight.

"It will help you connect to her."

The stone began to warm up in my palm. With a jolt, heat moved up my arm and I gasped, dropping the stone to the ground.

"Aria, no!" He hit the ground, frantically patting the hay for the small, now effectively invisible, stone.

"Crap. Sorry." I winced. Kneeling beside him, I began to move the tall strands of hay aside to help find the stone.

"She's going to kill me," he mumbled as he pushed the hay back.

"Who?"

"Runa. The dreamwalker. She's moody."

"Great." Of course she was. Today kept getting better and better. Luckily, it didn't take long to find it, but only because there was a connection to the stone I couldn't fight. "Got it!"

Astor tossed his head back, letting out a long, overly dramatic sigh.

I spit on the rock and shined it on my pant leg, much to his disgust. "What? Good as new." I held it up triumphantly, appreciating how it sparkled again.

"Just don't. Please."

"Okay." I shrugged, dropping the stone in my pocket. I didn't know if I'd use it, but it seemed important to him so the least I could do was take it.

"Let's go, kids."

I'd nearly forgotten Sade and Iri were there until her impatient command reminded me.

They were nearly a hundred feet ahead already, and Astor hurried to catch up.

I hung back, uneasy about what a strange dreamwalker could possibly want to talk to me about. It wasn't like I was good at controlling my powers yet. I had a hard time turning my thoughts away from the feel of the stone in my pocket as I followed slowly, its presence weighing heavily on me the rest of the way home.

CHAPTER 3

"Who asked you to come back?"

Damour's voice floated out from the kitchen window as I returned from dropping my friends at a tavern for the night. He sounded angrier than I'd heard him since childhood, when I'd broken his favorite toy.

It was so unexpected, I ran to the house quickly, worried someone had broken in. I flung open the door, pulling my knife from my belt as stepped into the kitchen. But when I saw my oldest brother, Harov, standing next to the fireplace, I put it away. Glancing between the two men uncertainly, I wondered whose side I was supposed to be on.

"What's going on here?" I hadn't seen him for many years and wondered if he even knew who I was.

"That's your sister, Aria. Talk to her because we're done here." Damour threw the washcloth on the floor and walked out, slamming the door behind him so hard a picture fell off the wall.

I bit my lip, hoping it hadn't broken, then tilted my head to focus on my estranged sibling.

"I knew who you were." He looked out the window, moving

to stand where Damour had been. He seemed unable to look me in the eye, and for a moment I wondered why.

Then it all came back—the day he'd left home.

I'd been barely five and had no idea what he was doing with his bags packed by the door so early in the morning.

He'd been startled when I asked where he was going but had recovered quickly. Ruffling my hair, he'd assured me he'd be back within the week.

It had taken me days to tell my parents, and by then, it was clear he wasn't coming back.

"It's been a while." I walked over to the table and took the seat by the window, gesturing to the one across from me. "Sit."

"It has." He perched on the edge of the chair, like he was prepared to bolt.

I noticed his eyes dart around the room as if he'd never seen any of it before, and remembered it *had* been two decades since he'd left.

He probably hadn't seen most of it.

I waited for him to speak, but it was hard. I had so many questions, the least of which was where he had been all this time.

We'd heard many things over the years, but there had been no way to know where he was, or even if he was still alive. And now here he was, looking like a younger version of Father, or an older Gavin.

When he remained silent, I prompted him. "Have you seen our parents yet?"

"Not yet. Damour said they're still in the fields." He shifted as he spoke, looking uncomfortable at my mentioning them.

I watched him intently, looking for clues about his life. It was true we shared parents, but I wasn't sure I would have recognized him if we passed on the street.

His skin was smooth and a pale alabaster, suggesting he no longer worked outside. His hands were clean, the nails trimmed short and filed. Even his clothing was clean, too clean, as if he wore something new every day. His boots were a soft, grey leather, buffed almost to a shine, with silver clasps for decoration.

I didn't have a sense of what his life was like, other than he appeared to be doing quite well for himself.

When he still didn't volunteer any information, I stood up in a huff, pushing back my chair as I went to the sink to compose myself. I poured a glass of water and took a few deep breaths, looking out the window as I centered myself. Once I felt calm again, I turned to regard him quietly for a moment.

"I'm not sure if you'll be welcome here." It was harsh, but true. I'd only been gone a short time, but I clearly wasn't welcome in town anymore.

"When I heard about everything, I came back. I hope that counts for something."

I rose an eyebrow, but he was looking at his hands. I took a sip from my glass, then sat down across from him again. I scoured his face, remembering the younger version, trying to see him in the stranger in front of me now. Much had changed, but his eyes were the same.

"What did you hear, exactly?" I was curious if he'd heard about me and if news of the prison break had spread.

"Enough to know to come home. Is it true? Is he here?"

I nodded, hurt welling up despite my efforts to remain calm. The only reason he was home was because of Beru, not because he wanted to help his family.

Damour returned with an armful of wood, glaring when he saw Harov was still present. Ignoring him, he addressed me instead. "Can you tell your guest to leave?"

"Tell him yourself." I stood, unwilling to take sides even though Harov's monosyllabic responses were starting to wear on me. While I hated he had deserted us, I'd always felt there was more to the story. And after the past few months, I was in no place to judge anyone.

Damour threw a piece of wood onto the fire. "Tell him we don't need his help."

"We don't need your help," I repeated, moving into the living area to watch them interact from a more comfortable perch.

"You do need my help. I know it will take time, but I'm here for the family now." He stood and walked over to Damour. "You've got every right to be mad. But don't let your ego hurt the farm."

"Hurt the farm? What do you know about our farm? You haven't been here to work the fields in many years." Damour brushed past him—hard.

"We could use the help around here," I interjected.

"So, what? I have to babysit Beru and now this idiot?"

I needed to get away from them and everyone. I was tired of defending Beru and no one listening. I stood and walked down the hall, leaving them to figure things out for themselves.

When I got to my room, I pulled out the stone Astor had given me. It shone brightly even without the suns making it sparkle. I ran my fingers over its smooth edges, intrigued by the craftsmanship. As I pulled my hand away, a zap of energy followed, causing the faintest sound of crackling in the air.

I placed the stone carefully on my night table, worried just by holding it I might already be connected to Runa. But it sat on the table, inanimate, and I snorted at my crazy thought. Lying back on the bed, I turned my head to make sure it hadn't budged, then looked up at the ceiling. Should I tempt fate?

Surely another dreamwalker wouldn't want to hurt me. If she'd been chosen as the next dreamwalker for the Western March, she'd likely been handpicked by Svan. What harm could come from a dream meeting with her?

I reached over, grabbing the stone before I could change my mind, and placed it on my stomach. I had no idea how to use it to connect with her, but assumed contact was important. I closed my eyes and let my mind wander to the Western March.

I immediately sank into a deep dreamwalk, finding myself in a large white room surrounded by windows. My feet carried me to the center of the room where two large white pillows had been placed on the floor across from each other. I sat down on one of them and crossed my legs.

As I waited my mind raced.

Was it a trick?

No.

No one could convince Astor to trick me intentionally, and he was too smart to be tricked into something that could hurt me.

I closed my eyes, already beginning to regret coming. Maybe I could get back to the farm before anyone noticed I was walking.

"Thank you for meeting me." Her disembodied voice reached me first, a magical, silvery sound which seemed to echo in the white space.

"You're welcome." I turned to see a woman with long blonde hair practically floating across the floor. Her grace was beyond anything I'd seen in a human, and her beauty was nearly enough to paralyze me. I had to blink a few times to make sure I was really there.

"I know this must seem a little weird for you, having only ever known one other dreamwalker." She sat on the other pillow and crossed her legs.

It was as if she'd come into sharper focus, and I realized she was younger than me. It was hard to look away, and I didn't know if it was magic or the commanding look on her face. I tried to shake off the feeling and forced a reply. "A little."

Runa smiled, a mischievous look in her eyes and placed her hands on her knees. When she gazed into my eyes it was like she'd found the place my deepest, darkest secrets were kept. Then she winked. "I promise this won't hurt."

I laughed nervously.

Astor's comment about her moodiness resurfaced in my mind.

Was this Runa in a good mood? She was still unsettling in a way I couldn't put my finger on, other than knowing I didn't trust her.

"Thank you for the stone," I was having a hard time putting two thoughts together in her presence, like I was being blocked somehow. Was it by her?

"Let's cut to the chase. I'm not one for small talk." She snapped her fingers and a box appeared next to us.

"Wow, you can do that as a dreamwalker?"

"Yes. You can't?" She lifted the top off the box.

"No." I marveled at her abilities; a tad jealous of how advanced she was.

"I'm sure you have some idea as to why I've called a meeting with you." She removed a pot from the box, placing it on the floor between the two pillows.

I was fixated by her every move, unable to look away. "I could guess why."

She was about to remove the lid from the pot when she stopped, tilting her head to look at me with an intense curiosity. "How's he doing?"

It made me uncomfortable, but I shrugged. "As well as can be expected. Gaining weight and strength."

"How was it in the prison? I've always wanted to know. Not badly enough to attempt to go, of course." Her smile dissolved into a stone-cold expression, her eyes becoming flat chips of ice. It was easy to see she disapproved. At least it was beginning to make sense why she'd wanted to meet with me.

"It wasn't pleasant." I didn't volunteer details, not wanting to give her any more ammunition against me if she was going to tell me how badly I'd messed up.

"Hm." She cocked her head, looking at me with narrowed eyes. "In any event, it happened. Unfortunately. And now I have to fix it." Her tone was cold, her eyes black.

I shifted uncomfortably in my seat. "Fix what?"

"Your little stunt." She finally lifted the top off the pot.

Smoke began to rise, and the air in the room became stifling with the scent of wood, betony, and elder filling my nostrils. The smoke began to form and project images.

I immediately recognized the inside of the prison and shifted uncomfortably. I didn't want to be here anymore, but I had no recourse except to wait for her to tell me why she was doing this.

"You know what you're looking at. This is the prison. Something's a little different than it's supposed to be. Care to guess?" The dry sarcasm in her voice made me uneasy.

I swallowed hard before replying, my throat suddenly dry from the smoke. "Beru is gone." What did she want from me? We were dreamwalkers. Shouldn't we be on the same side?

"Good guess. Try again." She crossed her arms, staring at me.

Increasingly angry at the cryptic interrogation, the strange sense of being unable to control my thoughts and speech vanished. I was done playing whatever game she was setting up.

"Let's cut the small talk," I stated boldly, a tingle of pride at her surprise replacing some of the anger.

"Let's. There's a hole ripped in the prison where you pulled Beru out. Do you know what that means?"

I opened my mouth, but she cut me off, her voice no longer sweet and silvery, but sharp and harsh. "It means anyone can leave the prison. Everyone can leave." She placed the cover back on the pot and returned it to the box. With a snap of her fingers, the box disappeared as if it had never been there.

I swallowed hard. I'd had my suspicions the hole hadn't

closed, but I'd been trying hard not to dwell on the possibility. I'd hoped once enough time passed and no one escaped everything would be fine.

She was confirming my deepest fears, and my guilt compounded.

I had wanted to forget it ever happened, but it appeared that wasn't going to happen. "Who else knows about the hole?"

"A select few, and now you." She placed her hands on her knees again and focused all her attention on me, waiting for a reply.

"How do we fix it?"

"We? I'm still debating whether I'm even going to take you on. I've been enquiring about you, and so far, I've been less than impressed. An unsuccessful career as a healer. An irresponsible response to being a dreamwalker." She shook her head regretfully, then snapped her fingers.

A servant appeared beside her with a tray of drinks.

She placed one in front of me.

I hesitated to pick it up, answering her charges first instead. I still didn't know if I could trust her. "I'm more than that. I know I've made mistakes, but I've been diligent in my studies since freeing Beru."

She followed my gaze to the drinks, and burst out laughing, a surprisingly deep, throaty sound compared to her voice. "I'm not trying to kill you. If I wanted you dead, I'd be more creative."

"That's very reassuring." I sat calmly, holding eye contact with her to show her I wasn't afraid, but didn't reach for the drink. I wasn't a fool, and we weren't friends.

"The prison is split now. Soon, darkness will be upon us. There's not much time. So, while I don't like it, it looks like we'll have to work together to have any chance at success." She picked up the other glass, slammed back the drink, then closed her eyes as she swung her head from side to side in appreciation of whatever had been in the glass.

"What if I don't want to help?" I sniffed my drink before taking a sip. I wanted to show her she didn't scare me. Surely if she could drink hers, mine likely wasn't poisoned. Probably.

"There's no *want* here. While you didn't free anyone else, others will find a way out of the prison. We don't have much time to fix the rip."

"How do you know others will find it? If they don't know it's there, they won't be looking." I placed my almost-full cup on the floor, well aware it was a sign of ingratitude to my host.

"My seer foretold it." Her eyes followed my cup to the ground, and she picked it up and drank the rest. "I don't like to waste."

I leaned back as far as I could, adding only a few inches of distance.

"We need to fix the prison now."

"And how do you propose we do that?"

Runa didn't have time to answer.

I heard my name being called far off in the distance. It quickly became louder, and my body began to shake. I closed my eyes and jolted up straight. An intense migraine gripped me as I struggled to pull away from someone.

A man.

I could feel his callused hands on my arms gripping tight and shaking. I came out of my dreamwalk breathlessly to find Beru standing over me.

His face was paler than usual, and his eyes had an edge of panic I'd never seen. "We're under attack!"

CHAPTER 4

The shifter's sword scraped against my bicep, forcing me to shift into survival mode.

Letting out a scream, I channeled the fierce energy rumbling from the pit of my stomach into the sword and plunged it into his scaly, green chest.

He fell over.

I jerked my sword out with a sickeningly wet sound.

I glanced at Beru just in time to watch as he finished off another lizard-shifter.

His fighting was so smooth it appeared choreographed, and I was so enthralled I almost missed the shifter approaching me from behind. At the last minute, the footsteps thundering toward me caught my attention and I turned, lifting my sword and preparing for battle.

She was shorter than the others attacking us, but I knew it meant she'd likely be faster, not easier to kill.

I'd never seen shifters like these before.

They had scales like the freshwater lizards I was familiar with, along with the same wide mouths full of razor-sharp teeth, but they fought upright like humans, which made many of them almost six feet tall.

This one was only about four feet, but her well-muscled arms were larger than mine even with my height advantage, and her shoulders were broader than mine by at least a foot.

As our swords clashed, I sensed Beru's eyes on my back, but tried to ignore the distraction. As I'd suspected, the tiny shifter was more than a match for me and I needed to focus all my energy on her if I didn't want to lose.

With each clash of our swords, my arms trembled and weakened. Sweat began to form on my brow, and more than ever I regretted not keeping up with my training since we'd returned to the farm. I'd been foolish to assume it would be a long time, if ever, until I was in battle again. Instead of watching Beru regain his strength through practice, I should have joined him.

The shifter's eyes darted just over my head, and I turned to see an enormous shifter join.

My eyes widened as I took in my attackers. No way I'd be able to fight both together. My pulse rushed in my ears as fear threatened to paralyze me. But even as I felt my luck had run out, Beru joined me, swinging at the larger shifter. With one last lunge, I swung my sword and sliced through my enemy's neck.

Her hands covered the wound, futilely trying to staunch the dark, algae-colored blood. Before long, she stumbled and fell to the ground, unmoving. Dead.

I turned toward Beru as the larger shifter fell in two pieces to the ground. He was breathing faster than usual, and covered in the dark green blood of his vanquished opponents, but otherwise appeared uninjured. Relief filled me even as I bent against my knees, sucking air.

"Are you okay?" He sounded concerned, but otherwise reassuringly solid.

"It's been a while." I huffed, still leaning over. I wondered if I would vomit. Ugh.

"Stay near." He placed a hand on my shoulder, patting it once before he spun on his heel and ran toward his next target.

My eyes moved toward the yard in front of the house.

Both Damour and Harov were fighting.

I could still see at least twenty shifters.

We were incredibly outnumbered.

A roar came from my left and I whirled to see a wolf, teeth bared, spring at me.

I side-stepped and almost avoided it. I lifted my sword but at the same moment, the claws slashed through my pant leg.

"Damn it!" I looked down to see blood seeping out of the scratch, and felt it begin to burn as the wolf-shifter's poison entered my bloodstream.

"Get to the house." Beru pushed me forward as he plunged his short knife into the heart of the beast. "You need to heal yourself now, before the poison takes hold. You're no good to us otherwise."

I nodded, darting back to the farmhouse. Once inside, I rummaged through the cupboards to find the items I needed to heal myself. He was right. I could already feel the poison weakening me.

I found the containers of dried *prunella vulgaris, achillea millefolium,* and *Symphytum officinale.* Throwing them on the counter, I reached down to where the pots and pans were and rummaged for my mortar and pestle, feeling a growing sense of urgency.

I didn't have long until the effects of the poison overcame my body and I was fast becoming frustrated at the state of the kitchen as fatigue began to creep through my body.

Typical of the way Damour did everything, there appeared to be no rhyme nor reason.

"Aha!" I placed the mortar and pestle on the counter, quickly placing a full pot of water to boil over the fire, noticing my hand shaking slightly. I returned to my impromptu work counter, carefully measuring out what I hoped was enough of the medicinal herbs for my leg, as well as extra in case there were more injuries.

Grinding the herbs to the right texture, I added them once the water was at a rolling boil. I stirred them to the right ten times, then to the left. Once the smell was uniform, I removed the mixture from the fire and poured some back into the pestle, grinding the liquid in with the remainder of the powder.

Panic rose in my chest as I applied the salve to my wound and waited. When the relief wasn't immediate, I wondered if I'd screwed up. Had I added the right ingredients? I patted another layer of the paste onto my other scrapes, and waited longer.

Still, nothing happened.

The skin around the wolf scratch wound was red and swollen still, the paste covering the marks from view. I collected cold ash from the edges of the fireplace and drew a circle around the wound, at the edge of the red skin. This way, I would be able to see if the wound was enlarging or contracting.

As I waited, certain I'd failed creating the healing paste, I glanced out the window.

Beru and my brothers were holding their own against the shifters.

I itched to get back there but my leg chose that moment to object as a sharp jab of pain made it tremble. Fatigue rolled over me, making it difficult to support my weight, let alone allow me to fight. I pressed my lips together and held onto the counter.

After what seemed like an eternity, the pain lessened. At first it was almost imperceptible, then gradually, my leg stopped trembling and I felt less unstable. I looked down to see the edges of the scrape beginning to close. "Oh, thank Suun!"

The redness had begun a rapid retreat from the edge marked with ash, so I grabbed a clean cloth and wiped it off, then wrapped it tightly around the wound and secured it in place. I checked the smaller cut on my arm, but it wasn't red or deep, so I left it to deal with later.

I ran out the door toward my brothers and my eyes met with the slimy barrier of a slug-shifter directly in my path.

It had noticed me and changed directions.

My heart sank. Its slick skin would be hard to penetrate, and the intense odor already stung my eyes from several feet away. The stench alone was bound to make it harder to fight him, even without the slippery, tough hide blocking my sword.

I took a swipe but missed by a wide margin.

Unfortunately, the single misjudgment allowed the slug-shifter time to jab at the wound on my arm.

I winced, trying to ignore the pain as I slid my short knife out of its sheath, aiming for the center of the unprotected soft underbelly.

Up close, my eyes watered from the overpowering stench, causing my vision to blur. I tried to pull back my knife, but instead of falling down, the slug leaned closer and wrapped a single flat, sticky arm around my throat. To my horror, and increasing nausea, it lifted me up.

I dropped the knife, frantically tearing at the squishy surface as I struggled to breathe.

It didn't lessen its hold, seemingly oblivious to my efforts.

Changing tactics, I kicked repeatedly as close to the wound which still had my knife in it as I could. My foot contacted the hilt, landing a lucky blow which drove it in further and caused the shifter to grunt.

His grip loosened enough I was able to get my hands between his arm and my neck to pry it off.

I fell to the ground and searched for my sword. When I spotted it underneath the single large foot, I held my breath and yanked, then swung it in the air as hard as I could and decapitated it.

There was no time to recuperate. Another shifter was at

my side instantly. It seemed obvious I was marked as the weakest fighter, and the remaining shifters were moving toward me.

Beru and my brothers saw the change in focus and fought their way to my side.

We fought together in a loosely clustered circle, backs in the center for several minutes until dizziness overcame me. I leaned over and vomited.

"Dragon dung. Sorry guys, I was trying to avoid that."

"That's your body getting rid of the poison. Don't fight it." Beru placed his arm around my shoulders as he whispered in my ear, voice low so the shifters couldn't hear.

I hoped he wasn't just trying to make me feel better. I vomited repeatedly, shoulders heaving as I tried to stop.

He faced our opponents, keeping his sword arm ready while I clung to the steady feel of his other arm supporting me.

My brothers took up points around me, forming a triangle as each fought a separate shifter.

My eyes welled with tears of frustration. As my vision continued to blur increasingly more from a combination of moisture and approaching unconsciousness, the ground shifted beneath me. The sound of swords clanking was tinny and distant, but I fought the oblivion of passing out. Taking several deep breaths, I wiped my eyes and gritted my teeth.

I looked at the wound on my leg, touching it lightly. Good. It had cooled considerably. Picking up my sword as I stood, breathing shallowly, I felt ready to return to the fight. The protective wall of men couldn't prevent that.

I attacked the first shifter I could reach, slashing through its armor just enough to catch its attention.

This one looked like an octopus, and the suction cups on its skin latched onto my sword.

I pulled hard, but my sword stuck was fast. I only had my short knife now, so I needed to pick the one blow which would kill the shifter. Then I saw the unprotected swatch under the bulbous face. Its neck.

I pretended to attack its mid-section, changing direction at the last moment and striking out at the neck. I growled when my knife bounced off the thick skin.

The shifter changed color and lunged.

I stepped back just as Beru sprang in front, easily slicing through the shifter's torso.

He retrieved my sword, handing it back. "You're too weak to do this."

His comment and the pity on his face made me want to fight more. Who was he to tell me what I could and couldn't do?

"I'm fine." I launched into my next attack, swinging my sword at a cat-shifter, slicing an arm off.

How was that for too weak?

The shifter swiped at me with the remaining arm, so I swung again, and relieved him of it. He brought his head forward and smacked it into my forehead, knocking me down. This time, I saw stars.

Beru stepped in front again, cutting the shifter in half with another easy swing before kneeling to look at me. His cool hand swept along my cheek up to my forehead.

I opened my eyes to see four of him looking at me. "You look really good in multiple." I closed my eyes, moaning at the pounding drums which were drowning out my ability to think.

"Is she okay?" Damour glanced down.

I tried to smile reassuringly at him, but my eyes kept closing. The ground felt so soft I didn't want to move. It hurt so much.

"She's not far from passing out," Beru sounded angry.

I tried to open an eye, but it was too bright.

"Aria."

I heard my brother calling, but I couldn't respond. The drums were louder now.

"Harov, stay with her."

Beru's energy disappeared as my brother took his place. I felt strangely sad, like I'd lost something precious.

"Can you hear me?" Harov whispered, his breath tickling my face.

"Yes," I muttered. It was too hard to open my eyes as the pain crested, an ocean of torment washing over and through me.

"We'll get a healer. Don't worry." He patted my shoulder, remaining at my side.

I lay on the ground for what seemed like forever, keeping one hand on my forehead and the other over my heart. When each clang of a sword echoed, I used what little energy I had left in an attempt to manage the agony. Eventually, I felt well enough to sit up, much to my brother's dismay.

"Please rest." He tried to push me back down.

"I'll be okay. I've healed myself the best I can for now, but we need to fight. We have to help them, or none of us will make it out of this." I stood, wobbling a fair bit, even with his help. I needed to fight better, smarter. This was my last chance to show them what I'd learned. How much I'd grown. That I was valuable.

I rejoined them, avoiding Beru's gaze.

His eyes had narrowed, and his mouth had hardened into a thin line. It was easy to see he wasn't pleased.

As much as I wanted to prove my worth, I knew he was right to worry.

Using my knife, I attacked the closest shifter.

Focused solely on my brother, it never saw me coming. Before he could turn, I slammed my short knife into his throat, and he dropped to the ground.

I moved on to the next shifter, another slug. I already knew the skin was tough and I'd need more force than normal to break through, so I didn't make the first move. She mirrored my movements, dancing with me in a slow circle.

A high-pitched battle call sounded and the shifters retreated.

The slug-shifter I'd been facing off against left, running in a strangely smooth, yet awkward gait from the farm with the others, leaving us alone.

Somehow, we'd won the battle.

"Is everyone okay?" Beru looked at the three of us.

My brothers nodded, then all three turned what felt like disapproving gazes to me.

"I'm wounded, but fine. I'll be able to heal myself. See?" I reached for the shifter-inflicted injury on my leg and ripped off the cotton bandage. It had healed, leaving only a small bruise in its place.

"Let's get inside." Beru didn't acknowledge my statement, walking toward the house instead.

We followed a few steps behind. When we got to the house, he refused to enter. "I'll stand watch just in case. You have enough to handle right now with your brothers."

I didn't know what he meant, but I could tell from his closed expression I wasn't going to convince him to follow. At least, not yet. So I opened the door and let my brothers enter, closing the door behind me.

I joined them in the living room, sitting carefully in the chair across from Damour, who was working methodically to stoke the fire.

Harov had elected to pace instead of sit.

We all remained silent for several moments.

He stopped, leaning against the fireplace as he crossed his arms. "Has this happened before?" He looked between us several times, his gaze resting on Damour when he answered.

"Yes, but they were ur'gels last time, not shifters. We were lucky this time," he added, not looking up from the fire.

"They took Denny from us," I whispered.

He hanged his head as he sat down on the edge of the couch. "I prayed that was a vicious rumor."

"This can't keep happening. If the others had been here, they would have tried to fight, and today would have ended differently. I have a child to consider now." Damour direct his comment at me.

The shock of what he implied made me turn from him.

Harov stood. "This is because of Beru."

"I didn't call them here. I don't want to fight. I want my life back." I crossed my arms, appalled at them.

"Damour is right. They won't stop coming."

"Why do you get a say in this? You're not part of this family anymore. You chose not to be." I felt my face flush as my blood boiled with anger. I leapt to my feet and balled my fists at my side. I was shouting now, but I didn't care. How dare he?

"I'm sorry. But I agree with Harov. You need to take him and leave." Damour looked at me.

Standing, I watched as tears filled his eyes.

He came over and extended a hand to me.

I dodged him, running to my room, I slammed the door behind me. All I'd ever wanted was my family together and safe at home. Now they'd turned against me. Choking back my heartbreak and compressing it into a hard ball in my stomach, I began to pack. If that's what they wanted, I would leave. And I'd never come back.

CHAPTER 5

I crammed what few belongings I had into a bag and left without speaking to them again. I couldn't imagine what I would say, and it pained me more than I wanted to admit when neither came after me to ask me to stay.

"Come on." I grabbed Beru by the sleeve as I walked out of the house, but he was like a mountain, and didn't move. "I'm leaving, with or without you."

"Where are you going? You need to rest so you can heal."

"I've been thrown out." My voice cracked, I jumped down the porch stairs, wanting to leave the house as quickly as I could, needing to leave before my last thread of pride frayed and I cried like a baby in front of him.

"What are you talking about? You're not making sense."

"Tell that to them. I'm a liability apparently."

Beru jogged after me, staying a pace behind.

I could feel his calm presence with me, but he remained silent. I waited a few beats, but when he still said nothing, I continued. "I'll never have a normal life again. After everything I've done for all of them, they threw me out. Like garbage. It's not like I asked for any of this."

When he still didn't speak, I turned, wondering if I was imagining him there.

"I've never taken you to be normal," he finally offered, pressing his lips together.

Irritated by his lack of emotion, I exhaled loudly. "Do you need anything? Because we aren't going back."

I crossed my arms and glared at him. For a moment, I wanted to yell at him like he was one of my brothers. I realized it wasn't fair. It wasn't his fault my brothers panicked the first time shifters attacked and blamed them on us. If it hadn't been for him, we would have died. With that in mind, some of my anger drained away, but it left the pain. That was worse.

"I have no possessions."

"Good. We'll go to the tavern. Maybe we can find Sade and Astor."

"Whatever you wish."

"You'll just go along with whatever I say?"

"You're the reason I am out of prison. I am indebted to you. Besides, it's not like I have anywhere else to go."

I speculated about whether he had been thinking about his family and what had happened to them and I felt guilty suddenly. Here I was, upset they didn't want me at home, but at least my family was still mostly alive. Now I was a whiner as well as an outcast.

"Where will we go?"

"I'm not sure, but as long as it's somewhere far away from here, it will suit me just fine."

"Astor told me about the dreamwalker in Western March. Maybe that's a start."

I wanted to laugh in his face, but that would invoke a conversation I wasn't ready to have with him. Not to mention Runa was almost the last person I wanted to see right then. She wouldn't welcome me with open arms to say the least.

"It's not an option." I snapped at him, deliberately keeping my tone harsh to avoid further conversation about the Western March.

"Got it." He picked up a stick and dragged it on the ground behind him, keeping pace but not arguing.

It pissed me off. I wanted a fight and he wasn't giving me one. But I also knew compared to what he'd been through I was acting like a complete brat. The logical part of my brain knew anything he said or did would annoy me.

My family was gone. Nothing would be the same now. Nothing. Not only did the townsfolk hate me, I'd lost my job as a healer, but now my own family had thrown me away. Everything I loved was gone. It almost made sense to throw myself into repairing the rip in the prison with Runa.

I stopped dead in the road. I may as well tell him. Get all the secrets out and maybe he'd leave me too. If I was going to be alone, why bother holding anything back? "We left a hole in the prison."

"So, others can escape?" He stopped walking, eyebrows raised as he watched me. The only thing giving away his feelings was the white-knuckled hand holding the stick. It was the liveliest he'd been since we left the farm.

"Yes." I continued along the path toward town, expecting him to catch up.

"We have to go back."

I turned around, incredulous he'd even suggest it. "I'm not going back there. They want nothing to do with me. They blame me for everything."

I threw my hands up in the air, almost jealous he had no one left. At least no one could hurt him anymore. I turned to stomp away, but I paused at the note which had entered his voice.

"To the prison, I mean. They can't be allowed to escape. You have no idea what they're capable of. No one alive has any idea." His voice was so gruff I could hardly make out the words.

I shook my head. "No one's getting out. Nobody in the

prison even knows they can. They've been stuck there for over two hundred years."

"If anyone knows I'm gone, you're wrong. They'll have been looking for a way out since I left." Beru walked past me, heading to town.

"Where are you going?" I was in charge, not him.

"To talk to Iri. He's the only one who'll understand."

"So, I'm not capable of understanding?" I placed my hands on my hips. Now he was irritating me on purpose, I was certain of it.

"You're young. You've been through more than most people your age, but you're still immature. You couldn't possibly understand what we're up against."

Fury coursed through me, and if I could have spit fire, I would have. "I saved you from a life of torture and this is how you think of me? Well, excuse this young, immature person for removing your ungrateful ass from your previous lovely accommodations. Next time, I won't."

"Please don't be mad. It isn't a personal judgment, it's just…" His words trailed off and his eyes widened as I stormed over.

I stopped an inch from his face. "Mad? Why ever would I be mad? It's not like I risked my life to save you, or lost everything defending you since." I emphasized my words by poking him in the chest every other word, before instantly feeling ill at the thought of spending any more time with him.

I couldn't believe this was happening.

The entire world was against me.

He didn't try to catch me this time.

As I came to a clearing, I looked back and couldn't see him. I didn't know if I'd lost him or if I even cared, but I slowed my pace to a walk to catch my breath. It felt good to run, even though everything still hurt from the battle with the shifters.

It wasn't far to the tavern, but I veered off the path into the trees to be alone for a little longer. I sat on a rock and took my off my pack, watching the water flow downriver. Closing my eyes, I listened to it burble on the rocks downstream. Something hit the water with a splash, and I spun to see a young boy fishing at the water's edge.

"Catch anything?" I placed my hand at the bridge of my eyebrows to shade my eyes from the sun.

"Why, yes I did, ma'am." The boy smiled back, nodding at the bucket next to him with pride.

I walked over to look at his haul, nodding once. "That's quite the take for one day. Your family will be very happy when you return."

"You look like that lady."

"What lady?"

"The bad one. The one who freed the demon." He turned and began to pack up his fishing rod and supplies.

"I'm not bad. I'm not what they say I am." I stepped back, uneasy about how afraid he seemed to be all at once. I guess news traveled fast.

"You shouldn't have done what you did." He grabbed the last of his things and, without a backward look, took off through the trees.

I bolted along the path away from him, running as fast as I could. It wasn't long before I had to stop and catch my breath again. The world as I knew it was unraveling before my eyes. Nothing was the same anymore.

I walked as fast as I could, too tired to run farther. I didn't even care what direction I was going anymore, I just wanted to be alone. Once I'd been someone everyone came to for help. Now I was shunned. But how could I regret saving Gavin? I knew even amid my pain I would do it all over. I could never allow anyone I loved to suffer without trying to fix things.

I wiped my eyes, and tripped over a large root. Luckily, my face stopped my fall. For a moment I lay still on the ground, uncertain if I should move. I was thankful for the pain. It was the first time since I'd left the farm a sensation other than anger had overwhelmed my self-pity. It was a nice change.

I slowly rolled over onto my back and stared up at the sky. The rusty smell of blood filled my nostrils, but I didn't heal myself. I deserved the pain, wallowing in it. It struck me maybe everything hurt so much because I'd forgotten what it was like to feel emotion.

When Denny had been killed, and the town attacked, I'd turned it off. It had been easier to cope with one task at a time. But now, I wasn't sure I was emotionally strong enough to deal with people's opinions of me. Maybe it was time to go back to that. After all, it didn't seem like there was anything I could say to make them understand how freeing Beru had been my only choice.

"This is a bit awkward." The voice came from the woods, and I froze.

I didn't need to look over to know who it was. Embarrassment at the possibility he'd watched me fall and lay there like a corpse made my cheeks burn, but I didn't move. "Not as awkward as it is for me."

He leaned against a tree beside my head, close enough for me to see the smirk. "Shall we head to the tavern, then?"

"I don't need any help." I struggled to stand, holding up a hand to stop him in case he offered, but when I glanced over, he seemed inclined to watch from his post at the tree.

He was kinda an ass, I decided, using my irritation to propel me forward.

We walked the rest of the way to town in silence, not even sharing a glance.

I kept my eyes to the ground, hoping no one would notice me.

Beru moved closer when we passed villagers.

If I hadn't known better, I would have thought he was trying to protect me. "We're here." I nodded toward a building.

He opened the door, motioning me ahead of him.

I took the stairs to the left of the bar and went to Sade's room. I knocked on the door.

It swung open. "It's too early for company." She noticed Beru and jutted her chin in greeting.

He gave me a strange glance, then turned and headed back down stairs as she opened her door wider for me to enter.

"Nice place." My eyes roamed the room, impressed by the feather bed and plush towels beside the ceramic wash basin.

"I'd rather be back in my cave." She went to the small table and poured us two glasses of water, offering me one.

I held my hand out, drinking it, then placing the empty glass on the table. "I'd like to leave. Today." I tried not to fidget.

Sade would see it as a sign of weakness.

I didn't want her to ask why, which meant short replies and no explanations.

"That soon?" Sade walked over to the window. "I'd go for that. I've been here long enough. I didn't think you'd be coming with me, though."

"I want to explore somewhere new." I tried to add excitement to my voice instead of desperation, but when she turned with one eyebrow raised, I knew I hadn't succeeded.

"Somewhere nobody knows your name?"

"Something like that." I'd been caught.

"He's coming?"

"Yes. He's got nowhere else to go."

She let out a sigh, grabbing her pack. As I waited, she placed all her items inside and took a last look around before smiling. "Shall we invite the boys?"

"Yes." I needed someone like Astor along.

He was always good-humored and quick to make light of situations. With my recent circumstances, I needed that more than anything else.

"I'd go wake him if I were you. You know that boy loves to

sleep."

I also enjoyed sleeping, as she very well knew. Not like I'd had a chance lately. But I took her advice and went across the hall to knock on his door. There was no response, so I let myself in. "Hello?"

To my surprise, he wasn't in the room.

His belongings were still there, so I knew he hadn't left.

I made my way back downstairs, wondering if he'd gone to get food, when I heard laughter floating out of the dining hall.

A smile curved my lips when I saw the three men seated together. Nearly empty plates had been pushed away from Iri and Astor. Beru had pulled a chair up in the aisle, leaning on the backrest with his arms while his legs straddled it on either side. Why did guys sit like that? I couldn't recall ever seeing a woman do that.

"Well, now I know where the troublemakers all are."

"And all at your beck and call, milady." Astor did a mock half-bow from his seated position. "So, I hear we're leaving?"

I glanced at Beru. What else had he told them? Shoving my annoyance down, I nodded. "You think you're up for it?"

"I'm up for anything!"

"What about you, Iri?"

"Where he goes, I must go," he grumbled. He appeared resigned, if not thrilled.

"Good. I'll meet you in the alley behind the tavern in an hour. I need to pick up provisions."

Before they could say anything else, I walked away. I knew they'd have questions and eventually, I'd have to come clean. For now though, the less said, the better. My only regret was having Beru know my secret when I didn't know if I could trust him.

In order for me to tell them about my family throwing me out, I needed to figure out how to deal with my emotions, or I'd be a soggy, sorry mess. All I'd ever wanted was to help people.

But how could I help when no one wanted me around?

CHAPTER 6

"That'll be five pounds of gold." The young boy held out his greedy hand, his eyes shining.

"We agreed on three pounds before." My hands moved to my hips as I gave him my best glare.

"It's not easy to get this many provisions so quickly. Especially when people suspect they're for you," he countered, unbothered by my indignation.

I dug deep into my pockets to retrieve the additional two pounds of gold, dropping them like they were hot onto the palm of his hand. "Now scram, you little maggot."

The boy skipped off without looking back.

I double-checked the list I'd given him. He'd gotten me a carriage with at least a month's supply of food as well as warm clothing, at least. I double-checked the other items, making sure he hadn't cheated me out of more than the extra two pounds.

"Traveling in style I see." Astor grinned as he and the others approached me. "Nice!"

"We won't be walking." I smiled for the first time, buoyed by the thought of a new adventure.

Sade jumped on the back of the carriage. "Where to now?"

I threw my pack in the back and considered the question. I had to leave, but had no idea where to go. The first decision was whether we should help close the rip in the prison. It seemed the obvious choice for a quest, and it might even help clear my name. If I could do that, perhaps I could come back and live with my family in peace. If they'd have me.

I jumped up on the back of the carriage next to Sade, pushing the sadness down. "I'm not sure."

"The Western March? Perhaps you and Runa could talk more. Who knows, maybe she'll mentor you." Astor looked at me eagerly.

I winced, pretty sure Runa wouldn't be interested in being my mentor. I was certain she hadn't told him the real reason she wanted to meet me.

After our brief meeting, as much as I wanted her to help me be a better dreamwalker, a larger part of me feared her. She was a very different person than Svan had been, and gave off the impression The Western March wasn't large enough for the both of us.

"Perhaps somewhere … different?" Beru locked eyes with me.

My stomach fluttered at the notion he knew what I was thinking and I looked down quickly, hiding the growing warmth in my cheeks. I waited to see if he'd say more, but Sade spoke first.

"That sounds ominous," Sade smirked, swinging her legs back and forth on the top of the carriage as she looked at him.

"The Western March makes sense. We're all familiar with it and I could take up my mentorship again as well," Astor insisted.

"If I could go to the Western March, I would." This was it. If I wanted them to come with me on this adventure, I'd have to tell them the truth. "The real reason we can't go to the Western March is because I've already had a dream meeting with Runa."

Astor's jaw dropped while Iri looked confused, but Beru remained quiet, watching me with his expressionless eyes.

My skin prickled at the attention and I turned gratefully when Sade broke the silence.

"I take it it didn't go well?"

"Not really, no. Her meeting had a definite agenda." All eyes focused on me, and I squirmed.

"I thought she wanted to mentor you, I swear." Astor looked devastated, as if his favorite dragon statue had disappeared.

I knew she hadn't shared her reasons with him, but I was nervous at the thought of breaking the real news to them, given its delicate nature. I didn't want them to regret their part in freeing Beru. "I know."

"So, what did she want?" She cut to the chase, looking impatient.

I glanced back and forth, unsure how well they'd take it when I told them. My stomach lurched and perspiration broke out over my entire body. I delayed my answer by taking my cloak off and folding it over my arm, smoothing out the wrinkles instead of looking at anyone directly.

"Does this have anything to do with the prison?" Iri spoke quietly, but with a calm certainty.

"Yes," I blurted, then waited for the next question.

But no one spoke. The silence grew to deafening levels as they blinked at each other and me.

I knew exactly how they felt. I'd give anything to go back to a time before I'd become aware of the rip in the prison.

"Spill it. I'm thinking the worst here." She shifted back and forth on her seat.

"There's no easy way to say it. I think I've suspected something all along, but I managed to repress my fears until she confronted me. She's a little frightening." I walked away from the carriage a few paces, giving myself a few moments to search for the right words.

"It's something bad, isn't it?" Astor scrunched his nose when I turned back.

"There is a tear in the prison where Aria and I left. It didn't close," Beru answered flatly.

After everything, Beru gave them the news, not me.

My mouth dropped at the way he'd taken over. How in Ash'gar had he done it to me again? I wasn't sure how to feel. On the one hand, it was irritating. I owed them the truth, I was the leader, but at least now it was out, which was a relief.

I watched their faces as they took it in.

Iri remained stone-faced, not unlike his usual appearance. Astor's face had paled, but Sade's eyes bored straight into me as if she was trying to read my mind.

I ducked away from her gaze, answering apologetically. "It's true. Runa asked me to fix the rip. No one has escaped or even knows it exists yet. But they could be looking for an exit if they know Beru got out."

Sade shook her head. "How is that even possible? Didn't you release him by dreamwalking?"

"I'm not entirely certain. We came through this tunnel. It was unlike any other dreamwalk I've had." I wished there were more answers for them, for me. It was just another example of me diving into something without having any idea what I was doing. I wish I could stop doing that.

"We can't let anyone escape. We aren't ready to fight them." Iri looked off into the distance, his voice low but steady.

"I know. I'm not sure how to close the rip though. Trust me, it's been on my mind ever since I spoke with Runa. She sort of gave me the impression I was a stupid child. I really don't want to ask for her help after that. We can figure this out ourselves. We don't need her."

"But she's a well-respected dreamwalker. Why wouldn't we ask for her help? She must have offered it if she wanted to meet with you," Astor reasoned.

I pressed my lips into a firm line as I looked at him. "I'm not opposed to working with her, I'm saying she doesn't like me and she won't help us. She's too busy working her own agenda."

Astor looked as if he would speak again, so I held up my hand. "You weren't there. You didn't see how she treated me. Runa doesn't expect me to fix this. In fact, I think she only met with me to tell me off and see if I had any information she could use."

"So, we'll head somewhere else. But where?" Sade jumped in, changing the subject before it became any more heated than it already was.

"Any other suggestions?" I looked at them in turn.

When no one offered a location, I jumped into the back of the carriage and began arranging our supplies, placing furs over the rice and corn so they wouldn't get damp and tying everything down to the sides so nothing would move or fall out the back. I kept myself busy for as long as I could, mostly to avoid answering any questions. I didn't want to travel alone. I hoped after some time to think they'd be willing to help me find a way to fix the rip. But at the same time, I hated the idea they'd think less of me because of what I had done. What I'd asked them to help me do.

I knew I would have to go back eventually, one way or another. The only other option I had was Runa, and I highly doubted she would be willing to help me after the way she'd acted in our dream meeting.

I tightened the straps on the end of the carriage. I'd delayed as long as I could. Hopping down from the back, I climbed into the front next to Sade, and waited. I didn't want to push them for an answer, but we needed to get going before it was too dark. I'd settle for someone just pointing in a direction.

"I think I have an idea where we can start. Somebody who can maybe help us." Beru finally spoke up.

"Can we trust him?" Sade raised an eyebrow, ignoring him as if he wasn't standing right beside her.

"I do." But I wasn't certain it was true. I wanted to, but was it my heart or head answering? If I was wrong, we'd all pay the price.

"Who is this person you speak of?" Iri turned to him.

Iri seemed to lack the reservations Sade had when it came to Beru.

I didn't know if it was a brothers-in-arms thing, or Iri's respect for a legendary warrior, but he seemed to trust him more than I did.

"She's the Light Woman. I don't know if she's still around, but when I was free to roam this world, she was the one charged with the keys to the prison."

"Can she be trusted?"

"I don't know. I can't guarantee she'll even help us. But it's somewhere to start."

"Does anyone have any other suggestions?" I looked at the others, but no one else volunteered an idea. It seemed this woman was our only other lead to repairing the prison. I knew they were here to follow me into battle, but this time, I wanted it to be their choice. Last time I'd been selfish and put their lives at risk to save Gavin. At the time I hadn't realized it, but now guilt over my previous actions made me worry I was influencing them without them truly understanding what we were planning.

"So, who's up for coming along? I want you to really think hard about your choice. This journey will be nothing like when we worked to free Beru. We'll be up against creatures we've never heard of, and may have to go places none of us have been. I can't guarantee anybody's safety, and this could be a one-way mission for some, if not all of us. I want you to do what's best for you. I won't think differently of you if you choose not to follow me."

As I watched them, my heart was in my throat. I'd told them my deepest fears, now it was up to them. I prayed Yina'ane'ut, the protector god, was watching over me now.

Sade placed her hand on my shoulder. "I'm going."

Even as my fear of being alone subsided, Beru's deep voice added to my relief.

"I'm with you as well. The rip is my responsibility, as much as it is yours."

"You'll need a wizard." Astor's voice was high and eager in comparison, and I hoped he understood the risk.

Looking at his innocent face, I couldn't help but fear he didn't. Still, it was gratifying.

"I go where he goes. It is an honor to fight alongside each and every one of you." Iri's firm voice finished off the group vote.

They had all decided to come.

An overwhelming feeling of happiness overcame me. I'd had very few friends in my life, and during the hardest events I'd ever faced these four had arrived. I wouldn't have known what I would do if they'd abandoned me after my town and family had cast me out, too. Now I didn't need to wonder.

We were all in this together.

Clearing my throat of the lump which had gathered there, I turned to Beru. "How do we find this Light Woman?"

He motioned for Iri and Astor to move closer to the carriage, scanning the area for any eavesdroppers. When he didn't see anyone, he leaned in. "I've never seen her, only heard of her. She's not someone to be taken lightly."

"We're on our own to find her, then. What if I speak with an elder? Perhaps one of them has heard of her." Sade leaned into the rough circle, raising an eyebrow as she tilted her head.

I was running out of people to ask, especially now. Most people seemed to barely look at me. Runa may know something, and I debated arranging a dream meeting to ask her despite my reservations.

"I have a few secure contacts I can get in touch with. But that will take a few days at least. I'll leave a note now." Iri offered.

When I nodded, he turned and headed back to the tavern.

"I've got an old acquaintance in the village I can ask. While Iri's writing his contacts, I'll see if I can track mine down. I won't be long." Sade jumped down from the carriage and took off down the road, leaving me with Astor and Beru to wait for them to return.

It was clear whether I was comfortable with the situation or not, I'd be relying on Beru much more in the future. He'd proven himself loyal so far, but I couldn't read him.

Regardless of his intentions, I knew he wouldn't follow me forever. The last few days had demonstrated how easily he assumed command. He wasn't a follower and I knew he'd want to be a free agent, sooner rather than later.

I could only hope that time came after we'd repaired the prison, because I didn't know if I could do it without him.

CHAPTER 7

"**D**o you trust me?"

We were walking through the woods when Beru surprised me.

"I'm in the woods, alone with you, on my way to see a witch because you recommended it. What do you think?" I stayed a pace ahead, not in the mood to go down that particular road. I wasn't sure if he could see my facial expression, but I was certain it would be irritated if he could.

"That doesn't really answer my question."

"Let's just do this."

I heard him sigh before he answered. "She's somewhere between four large trees. The doorway should be in a tree trunk."

The thought had already occurred to me he might have suggested seeing the Light Woman in order to free everyone in the prison. His sudden question had thrown me back to wondering if he would betray me.

I shuddered at the thought, trying to push it out of my mind. I had to believe he was on my side, that he wasn't the monster everyone thought he was. But it didn't seem to matter how many times I repeated it to myself, I couldn't quite shake the feeling he may have a different agenda.

"It's got to be here somewhere." He flattened out the bushes with his stick as he looked for the entrance, as if it would be easier to see without the smaller vegetation.

"Do you think she used a spell to hide the door?"

"It's possible. If that's the case, she probably knows we're here." He stood straight and looked around the area as if he was about to call out to her. "Isn't this your area of expertise? Aren't healers supposed to have a way with magic?"

I did have magical abilities, but my parents had worked hard to ensure I never used them. Just one more example of how I wasn't properly trained to do something. Magic wasn't the kind of thing you messed around with if you didn't know what you were doing. Gavin's accident had shown me that.

"If only we'd brought Astor."

"I'm not so sure about that kid."

"What do you mean?" An uncomfortable prickle slid down my back at his hesitation.

"He's too reckless for my liking and has a ways to mature yet, that's all. His intentions are good." He rubbed the back of his neck, tempering his statement.

I didn't reply.

He wasn't wrong, but it wasn't his place to speak that way about Astor. What was his fascination with maturity anyway?

We kept looking, though it was increasingly clear we had no idea where the witch was.

I walked to the river's edge, remembering a fairy tale my father told me about an elderly witch who lived along the water.

She often sank boats passing by and claimed the occupants as her slaves. The water was calm and peaceful. A slight breeze washed over me, and the smell of fresh water prickled my nostrils.

I closed my eyes as childhood memories came flooding back. The water fights we'd have after a long day's work in the fields.

Denny always finding a way to dunk each one of us at least once.

I held back the tears at the thought of him. I'd never see his loving face again, or get irritated when he poked fun at me.

He'd never dunk anyone again.

"Aria."

I looked back to where I'd last seen Beru standing before I'd gone down to the water, but he wasn't there, so I headed back toward where we'd entered the woods. I still couldn't see him anywhere.

"Beru!" I shouted as I jogged through the trees, fearful something had happened to him.

With my next step, I was flying. A net closed around me and I was launched into the air. Even as I began to process what was happening, the net reached the apogee and began to fall.

I shrieked as I braced for impact with the ground, wiggling and pulling on the thick rope for any give. As the ground rapidly approached, I gave up and closed my eyes, waiting for my life to be over. But the impact didn't come.

I opened my eyes in darkness, startled when I realized I was underground. I wobbled, slowly toppling over to land on the rich-smelling dirt. For a few moments I just lay there while my racing heartbeat slowed. Once it returned to a more normal rhythm and I could think again, I sat up. As I looked around, my eyes slowly adjusted to the darkness, but there was nothing.

"Hello?" I winced at the tremble I heard in my voice.

Silence.

"Is anyone there?"

A faint noise came from off in the distance, but I couldn't make it out. I focused on the location the sound seemed to originate from and a moment later, a flicker of movement rewarded me. As I watched, one of the shadows detached from the wall.

"I can see somebody." I tried to move, still trapped in the thick net.

The shadow drifted closer, and the ominous sound of chains scraping along the ground got louder. My heart raced. I wasn't able to fight, enmeshed in rope as I was. I tugged on the netting again, worried about what kind of creature was about to attack me.

"I'm not here to hurt you," I offered, my voice high, cracking on the last word as I frantically worked at the netting.

The shadow loomed nearer, the sound of its chains scraping louder on the Lynian floor.

My fingers suddenly found a hole in the net, and I pulled, releasing the top. Once the space was large enough, I jumped out and backed away until I hit the wall.

"Show yourself!" I pulled the knife out of my belt, feeling stupid I hadn't remembered it sooner. I could have been free earlier.

The noise stopped.

My heart pounded in my ears as I waited. "I'm not going to hurt you. Are you alone?"

I waited for a response. When it still didn't speak, I stepped forward. The shadow didn't move. I took a few more steps toward it. This time, it backed away.

"It's okay, you can show yourself. I won't hurt you."

I reached out my hand. Perhaps it wasn't the brightest move, but I needed to gain its trust.

The shadow came forward, the rattle of chains the only thing giving away its position. "Follow me." It sounded like a young male based on the childlike voice.

"Can you tell me your name?"

The chains moved away again. I had a split second to decide. Should I follow, or try to climb out of this hole?

"Aria." Beru's voice carried through the hole and I'd never been so happy to hear him.

"Down here!"

"Stay where you are. I'll find a way down."

I looked back to where I'd last seen the shadow. The sound of his chains had gone silent. I held in my frustration as I waited for Beru to make his way to me. I'd be safer with him by my side.

"Hurry," I wasn't enjoying remaining still in the darkness when I couldn't see my surroundings.

"I'm going as fast as I can. It's pitch-dark."

I tried to get a visual on him, but small branches and debris fell to the ground around me. Then a glimmer of light to my left caught my attention. That had been the same direction the shadow had run off in.

"Keep coming, hurry!" It took all my strength to stay put when every bit of me wanted to run after the shadow boy.

It wasn't long before Beru made his way into the hole, jumping to the ground beside me. Instead of the graceful landing I expected, he toppled over.

"Ow!" Through the shadows, I could see he was hunched over, his hands wrapped around his ankle. "I can't stand."

"Lucky thing, falling into a cave with a healer." Although it wasn't funny, I couldn't help making a weak joke to try to ease the tension.

I felt my way over and knelt beside him, placing my hands on his ankle. I closed my eyes, feeling his familiar energy as I felt the bones and muscles of the joint. Swollen, heat, but the bones were intact. Just a sprain. As I channeled my magic into repairing the damage, I tried not to enjoy his natural scent. A combination of trees and musk, fresh water and earth.

"It's working." He relaxed and leaned back, placing his hands on the ground to steady himself.

I kept my hands on his ankle as I worked, taking his pain away simultaneously. I felt connected to him in a way I couldn't explain, something which hadn't happened during a healing before. I pulled my hands away, embarrassed at my unexpected reaction and hoping he hadn't noticed.

Through the shadows, I watched him stand up. I wondered if he'd felt the connection, then told myself I was being foolish.

"There was someone here, a boy. I didn't see him very well, but he's shackled. I could hear chains when he moved."

"Could you make out where he went?"

"Yes, I was just about to follow when you called. It's this way." I grabbed for his hand in the dark, leading him into the tunnel. My hand tingled, but I ignored the sensation as we went deeper into the tunnel, following the faint light I'd noticed earlier.

He followed unquestioningly, his hand in mine.

As we approached the light source, our surroundings came into focus. The walls, ground, and ceiling were all green like grass, but different.

I reached out to touch the blades of grass, and they stuck to my hand. When I pulled away, my hand was covered by tiny scratches on my fingers where the grass had made contact. Careful not to touch it again, I moved cautiously.

The overgrown grass was difficult to move through. Other strange sights became visible as the light intensified. Small bugs in iridescent shades buzzed in the air, ignoring our presence as they flitted around, landing on strange, vibrantly colored flowers before taking off again.

"Anything in your healer book about this?"

"No. This is all new to me. Have you ever seen such animals like that one?"

I pointed toward a large yellow creature with four horns on its head. It rolled over on its back in a little pool of water and bleated adorably. It reminded me of the sheep on our farm, if someone had made them shorter, fatter, and dipped them in daffodils.

"Nothing like this. Let's keep going."

As we walked along, a slight movement in the lush vegetation caught my eye. When I turned, I saw a person walking along a rough path and I reached for Beru, pointing my chin toward the figure. "Look, over there."

His eyes sharpened on the shape of an elderly woman and we approached her cautiously.

The woman paused, but kept her back to us. Unkempt white hair hid her face from view so that at first, she seemed to be talking to herself. "I'm checking my nets to see if I've caught anything for supper. Are you hungry, too?"

I looked around, answering after a pause when I decided she was waiting for us to answer. "I am looking for a boy who came this way."

"Are you sure about what you saw?"

She turned around, displaying pale, blotchy skin as if she hadn't seen the sun for centuries, and a large, pointed chin to match her pointed ears. Her face was a map of wrinkles, but the eyes sparkled with curiosity, ageless and full of life in the otherwise wizened face. It was difficult to tell how old she was, but I knew elves could live many centuries. Maybe she would know something.

Wait, what had she asked me?

"Well, no. It was very dark," I admitted, confused. Maybe I hadn't seen the boy.

Something about the way she was watching me made me wonder if I was in a dream. After all, the plants and animals were unlike any I'd ever seen in my waking hours, and this elderly elf woman was the strangest I'd ever seen.

"What is it you seek?" Her eyes burned into me, searching, testing.

"You're the one we've come to find. The old witch." Beru seemed unaffected by whatever was making me feel muddled.

"I'm unaccustomed to company, but it's nice to have someone to chat with from time to time. Maybe a nice cup of tea." Her voice became thoughtful, and she waved her walking stick in the air. A door appeared in a large tree beside her and she smiled sweetly. "Follow me. My home is this way."

He bowed slightly, showing no hesitation as he followed, but I lagged behind.

Something about the entire situation was bothering me, but I couldn't put my finger on what. Was it her oddness? I was sure I'd seen the boy, but doubted my certainty.

Once inside the tree, the door closed behind me at another absent wave of her stick. She continued down a narrow hallway with a ceiling only high enough for her to stand easily, which meant I had to duck my head to avoid hitting it, and Beru had to stoop several inches.

We followed her farther inside, into a small, circular room which was pleasantly decorated with cozy chairs and cushions, complete with knitted blankets and stacks of books along the walls. But as with the hall, everything was perfectly sized for her, which was to say a little too small for an average adult human to be comfortable.

"My apologies, I'm afraid everything in my home has been made perfectly for myself and no one else. I do like it that way." She shrugged, taking in Beru's awkwardly bent form.

"It's fine. It's your home, so it makes sense it fits you best."

I bit back a smile at his politeness as the witch waved her hand in the air. I blinked as a pot with three cups appeared on the small table in the center of the room.

"May I offer you a drink? It's fish blood, my favorite for an afternoon snack."

"I'm good." I waved her offer of a drink away, gingerly moving to a nearby chair and sitting down carefully. It was barely large enough for my backside and I could only hope it would hold my weight.

"I'll have a glass."

I watched him with surprise as she poured him a glass and slid it across the table, watching him gleefully as he drank the fish blood like it was a glass of water.

"You surprise me. So, it is true, you have escaped the great prison." She poured another glass, eyes sparkling as she waited for him to drink it.

He placed it beside him, nodding calmly. "Yes. Now we've come to ask for your help."

"What is it I can do? And why should I help you?" She looked disgruntled when he didn't drink the second cup, but looked up to focus on his face when he replied.

"We need to know about the Light Woman."

"Oh, my! There's a name I have not heard in many, many years. And one I can't say I missed hearing."

I narrowed my eyes at her unexpected reply. Wasn't she supposed to be the one who knew where to find her?

"We need to know where she is. I was told you know the answer." His body had tensed, and I noticed his hand was hovering near his sword, though not yet touching it.

"The Light Woman was a High Elf in her time, always thinking she was better than others." She stood, taking the cups and pot off the table, and stalked over to the kitchen in a huff.

I could hear her muttering unintelligibly the entire time, and once she returned it was to cross her arms and glare down at him.

"I wish you luck finding her, but I'm afraid you're far too late. She's been dead for over a century." Just as quickly as she'd become insulted, she now began to cackle as if she'd said something hilarious, slapping her knee as tears sprang to her eyes.

I shared a confused look with Beru. Was she lying to us? What had we gotten ourselves into? First, I'd been trapped in a net and thought I'd seen a strange boy in chains.

When we finally found the witch, she'd offered us disgusting refreshments, and was completely unused to conversation with anyone, as if she'd been a hermit for centuries.

I just needed out. "Well, thank you so much for your time, and your kind refreshments. We'll just be going if you can show us the way?"

Her lips pressed into a thin white line. She crossed her arms, all traces of laughter vanishing. "Well, if you're going to be like that. I was thinking you could stay with me."

I stood quickly, almost losing my balance when I yanked myself out of the tight seat, and bowed as low as I could. "I am so sorry, but we need to leave. We are on an important quest. Please accept our apologies."

She marched over to the hall, waving her stick again. The crack of the door opening let a faint light into the room "Fine then. But once you exit, you cannot return. The door will be invisible to you unless I wish it to be seen. I'm not so sure I like you." She wrinkled her nose, glaring at me.

I swallowed hard.

She was just odd enough she may decide to trap me again, and I didn't want that. Rummaging through my pockets, my hand closed on a small quartz stone I'd found on the ground which I'd thought pretty at the time. Now I hoped it would tempt the strange and likely dangerous woman.

"Please, accept this parting gift. Perhaps it will be of value to you. I would be more than happy to visit again, once my task is accomplished. If ever you are in want of an afternoon tea with my company, of course."

The tense lines on her face smoothed out and she hummed with excitement, the way a child might on receiving a gift. She darted over, picking the rock out of my palm before dashing over to a corner to look at it under the dim golden lamp light.

"Ooooh, pretty!" she sang, dancing around as she looked at it. When she stopped, her face was again the sharp-eyed face of eccentricity, all traces of anger removed by the small gift.

I exhaled with relief. Something in my gut had been warning me the entire time. Whether the boy in chains had been a figment of my imagination or her prisoner, I was certain we were narrowly escaping an indefinite visit with the witch of the woods.

CHAPTER 8

I'd never been happier to see trees as when we exited the strange home of the even stranger witch Beru had taken me to see. As we walked back to meet the others, I couldn't help stealing glances at him when he wasn't looking.

He seemed unbothered by what we'd been through, his face the same blank, hard-to-read canvas. I knew he'd been through far worse in the prison, so it was possible his lack of reaction had more to do with his past than with not being worried, but it led me back into the same loop of uncertainty.

Could I trust him? Had saving him been a good idea? I was running through my now-familiar concerns when he broke the silence.

"We need to go to Bruhier."

"What?" For a moment, I was stunned.

He'd stopped in the middle of the forest path and looked at me as if I should already understand what he meant.

When I continued to stare at him blankly, he rolled his eyes.

"Bruhier is where the High Elves live. If the Light Woman is dead like the witch says, the likeliest place to find someone who knew of her is in Bruhier. Perhaps she passed the key down to a descendant."

What he said made sense, but the logistics were daunting. Bruhier was a continent composed of massively tall islands with plateaus where the elves lived, hidden by low-lying clouds.

"How will we get there? We would have to get above the veil, and I don't know anyone who's ever been there. Don't they have giants?" I knew I sounded scared when my voice cracked, but I didn't mind him hearing the fear this time.

Bruhier was a place almost as mythic as Suun's lost temple. While it was true the plateaus had a diverse population—including humans, elves, and other creatures—it was said to be an extremely difficult journey. Those living above the veil weren't known to take kindly to strangers. Rumor was they would just as soon kill you as talk to you.

He nodded. "Yes, there are giants. At least, there were the last time I was there. I know a way, if you wish to go. We need to head west, toward the coast. From there we'll have to hire a boat to get to the islands."

It sounded simple enough, and we didn't have another direction, now that the witch hadn't panned out. "Okay, but only if the others agree. Bruhier is another commitment altogether."

THE CONVERSATION WENT BETTER than anticipated. In fact, I was the one with the greatest reservations. It seemed once they'd decided to sign up for this adventure, it had been a blanket agreement. With only faint grunts of acknowledgement from Iri and Sade, and the expected excited bouncing from Astor, we set course for the western coast.

We traveled for the rest of the afternoon, setting up camp just before nightfall.

Iri dropped a deer from the carriage with one shot from his

bow about the same time, securing dinner. He jumped down and began to prepare it while Sade and I gathered firewood.

Beru enlisted Astor to set up the rest of the camp. From the interactions I caught while going back and forth searching for kindling, it was apparent Astor wasn't exactly helpful. Beru took it in stride, without any outward irritation. As silent as he was, I thought I was beginning to get glimpses into the kind of man he must have been before his imprisonment.

He was patient with those he saw as young or inexperienced. However he valued Iri as his equal and respected his skills. More than once he'd commented on mine or Astor's immaturity, which irritated me enormously, but when I was honest with myself, I knew he was right. Even so, he'd never used it against me, except for when he was acting protectively, the way my brothers sometimes did.

Sade reached over, gently shoving my shoulder with her hand. "How many times do I have to say your name for you to hear me?"

"Sorry, I've got a lot on my mind." I snapped back to my task and tried to light the fire by rubbing two sticks together.

Sade watched impatiently for a few moments before grabbing the sticks, rubbing them together more rapidly than I'd done. "You've never been good at that."

I wrinkled my nose. "Thanks, I guess."

"What's on your mind? The journey?"

"Yes."

"Okay, spill. What's really on your mind? Do I need to ask?" Sade raised an eyebrow, then turned her attention to the thin curl of smoke wafting from the kindling and began to blow on it gently.

"No, likely not. It's just … I don't know what to think anymore. I want to stop thinking about him, but it's hard to do when he's always around."

I sat back on my heels, hugging my knees as I turned slightly to catch a glimpse of him from the corner of my eye. Beru and Astor had gathered moss for us to place beneath our sleeping mats for extra cushion, and were now arranging them in groups.

"Why don't you just do the dirty and get it over with?"

She laughed at my expression, mocking me by opening her eyes wide and dropping her jaw slightly, before throwing a tiny branch at me.

Unable to find words, I threw it back instead.

She easily dodged, but when she saw my face, she sobered. "Go. Talk to him. Get to know him better so you can decide what you think. But don't expect anything. Eventually, he's going to want to lead his own life." She laughed humorlessly. "Heck, if I'd been sprung from a prison I'd been in for centuries, I'd run for days before I stopped to rest, let alone follow some strange woman without expecting or demanding anything."

"I know. I wish I could explain how I feel drawn toward him. Sometimes it feels like all I think of is him or the prison." I glanced back to find him staring at me and quickly turn away. Had he heard us?

"Go." She jerked her chin toward him. "Get it over with so the normal Aria can come back."

I didn't want to, but at the same time I knew she was right. I needed to decide for myself if he was good or bad, and until I did I was going to continue to go back and forth about whether I'd done the right thing by letting him out.

I got up while I still had the courage, walking over to where he was putting the finishing touches on the beds.

Sade called for Astor to come help her as I reached him.

I swallowed hard at the unexpected silence, awkwardly pointing at the pallet. "Looks like a comfortable bed."

He smiled, sitting down and bouncing slightly to test it. "Thanks. You looked intense over there. Everything okay?" He patted the spot next to him as he waited for me to answer.

I sat at the other end of the bed, keeping some distance between us. "Just strategizing."

"I'll have to take your word on that." He looked out at the water, and I realized he was quieter than usual.

"How are you doing? Being outside in the world again?"

"Living and breathing."

I bit my lip, wondering what to say in response. It was the first time we'd been alone without being in some sort of danger. It was awkward, but I had so many questions to ask. How did I begin when I had no idea what he was going through?

He spoke, interrupting my thoughts, his voice raspy. "I can't stop thinking about them."

"I'm sorry." It was so inadequate, but what else could I say?

He looked at the ground as he continued, and I caught the glint of the tears he blinked rapidly away. "I can't stop thinking about if they believed those who said I was evil."

"They knew who you were at your core." I sat stiffly beside him, unsure where to look or place my hands as I struggled with whether to sit with him or leave him alone with his thoughts.

"I don't even know who I am anymore. Being in prison for so long, forced to do things I never want to speak or think of again. Not seeing the sunlight for over two hundred years, and now I'm fighting the darkness when I sit in the sun." His shoulders slumped as he placed his head in his hands.

I slid closer, unable to watch his pain without trying to ease it. Carefully, I placed my arm around his shoulders. A pleasant warmth grew where it rested. "It's all over now. You're free."

"Free? What does that even mean? My mind isn't my own. Every time I close my eyes, I'm still trapped." He straightened, shaking off my arm.

I remained in place, but let my arm drop into my lap. "Then you have to change how you think."

"I don't know how to do that anymore. There's darkness inside me. Right now, I'm fighting to keep it locked away."

I remained quiet, feeling like an intruder on his personal thoughts.

When he got up and walked away without another word, I was certain he'd shared more than he'd intended to. Unfortunately, it didn't help me decide whether or not I could trust him. If he didn't know who he was, how could I?

"Are you eating or what?" Her harsh cry made me smile, stirring up memories of my mother yelling at us to come in from the field.

I got up and joined them sitting as far from him as I could. It didn't matter though, because his only focus seemed to be on the fire or his food.

"There's nothing like fresh meat," Astor stated appreciatively as he rolled his stick of meat over the fire, browning it evenly.

"Can't you just use magic and cook all of it with a snap of your fingers?" Iri rose an eyebrow, watching impatiently as the magician drew out the cooking experience.

"Ah, but that would be too easy. And you wouldn't have the marvelous experience of sitting around the fire with your friends while waiting for your meal," he tipped his hat gallantly.

"In other words, he has no idea how to do what you're asking," she teased, poking him in the shoulder with her finger.

He poked her back, sounding indignant. "That's quite a way to ruin a good evening."

"Now, now. No fighting." I joined in.

We all chuckled, except Beru, who wasn't paying attention.

He was still staring into the fire, apparently lost in thought.

I bit my lip wondering what he was thinking.

"What about you, Beru? What were your kids like?" She looked at me and winked.

My face flushed. Now he'd know we'd been talking about him for sure.

She shouldn't have known about his children.

He didn't speak right away. For a moment, I thought he wouldn't answer at all, then he exhaled slowly.

"Very young and innocent." His serious tone was the opposite of our previous light-hearted banter, and we all fell silent as we waited for him to continue. "They looked like their mother. But had my temper." He half-smiled, but it faded quickly.

"I'm sorry you lost them. You should have watched them grow." Iri clapped him on the shoulder with a hand, gripping, then releasing.

"Do you have any kids?" He looked at Iri.

He shook his head and smiled, a hint of wistfulness crossing his face. "No, I've not been fortunate to have a woman like me enough to marry me."

Beru nodded as he rolled his meat over the fire. "That surprises me. You're a good man."

"I'm really not. I just do as I'm told."

"Wow, this turned somber." She stood up, pulling her meat off the fire. "I think we're all pretty decent. Let's leave it at that."

"Even me?" Astor looked around, an air of hopefulness around him.

"At this moment." She poked his shoulder again with a mischievous look I knew well.

"What was it like in there?" He turned to Beru, ignoring her attempts to pester him.

Beru leaned back. "There's nothing I can compare it to. It's dark, cold, and lonely. Very lonely." He stood up and retreated to the beds, leaving us staring after him.

"Why did you ask him that?" I scolded Astor, trying to keep my voice low so Beru didn't hear.

"It was getting too sentimental. I've always wondered what it was like there and no one else knows." He shrugged, completely unaware of how insensitive he was being.

"Aria knew." She took Beru's spot by the fire and her steady gaze made Astor flush and look away.

My eyes trailed over to where Beru had lain down on the bed, almost out of earshot. "It's tough for him. We shouldn't be making him relive it. No more questions," I ordered the rest of the crew to leave him alone.

"Yes, ma'am." Astor saluted.

Sade immediately popped him in the shoulder.

"Ow! Can you please stop hitting me?"

"When you finally start using all of your brains, not just the ones running your mouth." She slapped him again for good measure.

I quickly finished my meal and excused myself, making my way over to the bed where Beru had disappeared. I lay down on the bed carefully, trying not to disturb him.

As a healer, I was able to pick up on people's emotions—not everyone though, only those I had a connection with. I closed my eyes and immediately a wave of intense sorrow pushed against me.

Unconsciously, I reached my hand out and placed it over his. Our fingers intertwined, and we remained like that. No words were required as I listened to his quiet sobs. I desperately wanted to heal his pain, but knew it would mean erasing the memories of his family.

So instead, I'd wait for him to tell me more. There was no way I could understand what had happened in that prison. It terrified me when I thought about being trapped there. But as his tears fell, I knew one thing for certain.

He may be silent, he may be hard to read, but he wasn't a monster.

I sure as hell wasn't a monster for freeing him.

"I'm sorry." His voice thick as he squeezed my hand.

"It's okay. You don't need to explain anything now. I'll be here whenever you need to talk." I squeezed his hand back but didn't look at him. I wondered if it was easier as the darkness fell to share his feelings.

"I can never be a free man again. As much as I want to. I've seen too much." His voice trailed off, but he kept my hand in his.

We laid in the deepening silence, the heat from his hand telling me more than mere words ever could as I took deep breaths to hold my own tears back.

I couldn't fix him, or offer him anything other than my presence, as much as I wanted to make it all go away.

"Don't give up on me," the pain-strained his voice, making it barely audible.

I closed my eyes and pretended to sleep, uncertain if I'd been meant to hear his last words.

His breathing gradually slowed, signaling sleep.

I wanted nothing more than to move closer and hold him while he slept.

There had to be a reason I'd been called to save him. A reason none of the other dreamwalkers had been led to his prison. The strange pull of gravity I felt toward him made me wonder if he'd been called on to save me.

CHAPTER 9

Dampness chilled me, causing me to wake with a start. I jerked up, smacking the back of my head on a brick wall as I moved. Wincing I stood, wiping down my clothing, shivering against the unexpected cold.

The last thing I remembered was falling asleep near Beru's comforting warmth. Now when I exhaled I could see my breath. I knew I was back in the prison.

My eyes slowly adjusted to the darkness as I scanned the room. A window along the back wall served as the only light source, allowing me to see I was standing beside a door. I tried to turn the knob, but it was jammed.

I moved to the back of the room silently, my mind filled with the vague notion of trying the window. Why couldn't I be in bed sleeping, having normal bizarre dreams? I needed to lose this awful connection to the prison as soon as possible. I'd already done what had been demanded of me when I'd freed Beru, hadn't I?

As much as I wanted to push it all away, though, I knew I'd keep returning until I figured out why I was here. My dreamwalking had to be connected to the rip somehow. If I could find out why I kept returning, maybe I'd figure out how to close the rip as well.

Once I reached the window, I searched for a way to open it, but it was sealed shut. It was easier to see the room with the increased light from my adjusted vision, so I examined my surroundings again.

I wasn't in a place I recalled seeing before. Strangely enough, it appeared to be a classroom. Several desks were arranged in neat rows and my mind whirled at the possibilities. What could they be teaching at the prison? Had Beru been part of this, whatever it was?

I searched in and around the desks for clues, but there was nothing. When I looked back at the front of the room, I noticed a dark shape looming in the corner for the first time. I stifled a scream, letting out a shaky breath when I regained my focus.

Not human, thankfully, nor creature. It was a large, triangular-shaped object much larger than the door, almost touching the ceiling. Carefully, I approached to examine it closer.

What was it and how did it get in here?

I ran my hands over the smooth surface, looking for a way to open it. There didn't appear to be a handle or lever, and I saw no markings to explain it. I knelt to feel the bottom and was able to see it was being propped on something. I ran my hand underneath just as the ominous sound of a door creaking open sounded from behind me.

I ducked, placing my body between the object and the wall, trying to make myself as small as I could, and waited for whoever had opened the door to enter. But only silence greeted my ears. I remained frozen in place, wishing I was invisible as panic set in.

The sound of the footsteps from the hallway echoed into the room. Someone *was* coming. My heart was now pounding so loudly I was convinced they would hear it. I placed my hand over my mouth to muffle the noise from my shallow, rapid breathing.

The footsteps were right outside the door now. I begged quietly for them to pass by.

But they stopped.

Right in front of the door.

As the door swung open, I squinted to see who or what was there, but it was empty. I forced myself to sit still even as I wished I could dreamwalk right out of there. I needed to stay, to find out what was chasing me and why I kept returning.

The door slammed shut, surprising a muffled cry from my lips before I could stop it. Energy had entered the room, the same energy I'd felt before. My hands shook against my face as numbness set in. It knew where I was.

A desk flew across the room, crashing into the wall with a deafening clatter.

I pushed myself even deeper into the corner. Closing my eyes, I tried to break free from the dreamwalk, but nothing happened. I was too drained.

The triangle-shaped object flew away, exposing my hiding spot.

I moved closer to it, but I knew it was hopeless.

It obviously knew I was there. There would be no more hiding.

Making a break for the door, I prayed I'd be able to exit. My energy was waning due to the force being emitted from the unseen being. I only hoped if I could get far enough away, I'd be able to break the connection.

I reached for the door. The handle turned and I slipped out, racing into the hallway as I ran for my life. My only plan was to put as much distance between myself and this energy-sucker as possible.

The farther I ran, the easier my breathing became and

slowly, I felt my energy return. I didn't stop, instead running faster as I tried to add more distance between us.

"I've been waiting for your return."

I glanced back, into an empty hallway. No one was there. I kept running.

"Run as much as you want. I can feel you, no matter how far away you get. I'll find you soon enough." A deep menacing laugh echoed, bouncing around in the darkness.

Without slowing, I screamed into the air. "Get away from me!"

"I'll find you. Soon." This time, the voice sounded like it was right in my ear.

I whirled, almost crashing into the wall as I spun, trying to see my stalker. But again, darkness met my eyes. No one was there.

The disembodied voice sounded again, only this time amused. It drew the next words out silkily, almost singing them. "I have a gift for you."

"I don't want it." My voice was barely a whisper as I tried to see who was speaking.

"I hope you enjoy it. You'll see what I mean soon enough." A deafening laugh rebounded off the walls, making it hard for me to think.

Covering my ears, I screwed my eyes shut as I tried to free myself. As my airway closed from the effort, I sat up abruptly.

I was in bed gasping, my heart trying to race out of my chest. I rested my elbows on my knees and sucked in as much air as possible until my lungs gradually expanded. I stayed there for what felt like ages, breathing in and out, and then his warmth was at my side.

Beru slung an arm over my shoulders. "Are you all right?"

"I'm fine. Just a bad dream," I wanted to keep my dreamwalking a secret. I didn't want to worry anyone, especially him, until I figured out why it kept happening.

"You kicked me in your sleep. I hope you weren't thinking about how mad you were at me." He leaned closer, giving me a nudge.

I smiled at his sudden playfulness, trying to push away the darkness. "You're safe. I was just doing farm work. I've always hated the chores Father gave me."

Beru narrowed his eyes slightly, pursing his lips as he considered my reply. I could tell he didn't believe me, but thankfully he didn't push. "You okay to try to get some more sleep?"

"Yes."

I laid back down, facing away from him. I couldn't sleep though. Even as my eyes burned with exhaustion, I made myself stay awake. I could feel him watching me, concern radiating from him, but I remained on my side. I couldn't share my concerns and I couldn't chance returning. I wasn't strong enough to escape there twice in one night.

When Sade slipped out of bed several hours later, I debated joining her at the campfire. Maybe if I told her about my dreams, she'd understand.

I heard Iri greet her and decided to wait, not wanting Beru to find out about last night just yet.

He was happier in the present and I worried if he knew what I was seeing it would bring back horrors he didn't need to experience.

I closed my eyes for a moment, lulled into a twilight state by the comforting sounds of the breakfast preparations. I wasn't sure how long I dozed, but Beru's hand on my back startled me awake. I did my best to remain still and appear to be asleep, but when he moved closer it grew more difficult to pretend.

"Are you awake?" He rubbed my back, a gentle shoulder to mid-back caress. It should have been completely platonic, even parental, but it sent tingles down my spine.

I didn't move.

He slid closer, the heat from his chest almost touching my back as he leaned over, whispering into my ear. "Are you hungry?"

His breath tickled, and I had to force myself not to squirm.

"I'm trying to sleep." I made my voice sound as gruff as possible. My reaction was bothering me, and I needed to put some distance between us.

"I'm going to get some breakfast. Want me to bring you back something?"

I shook my head but didn't turn it. "I'll get up soon. Don't worry about me." I closed my eyes again, hoping he'd take the hint without me having to say anything hurtful.

"I do." He paused. "Worry about you, I mean."

I didn't know how to respond. It was the first time he'd displayed anything other than his normal emotionless self when it came to me, and it confused me.

"Are you slackers going to get up? Daylight's a-wastin'!" Sade's strident voice shattered the fragile moment and granted me a reprieve.

"Coming." I slipped out of bed and away from him. When I touched my cheek, trying to cool the heat I felt, I wiped encrusted drool off my chin. Great. Just perfect. I heard the slap of his feet on the ground and knew he was following.

"We have venison, venison, and more venison. Take your choice." She smiled proudly as she held up a platter of shaved meat.

I picked up my plate, scooping a fair amount onto it, then moved to sit next to her. He took the rest of the plate and sat beside Iri.

"We should start cleaning up soon. I want to get in as many miles today as possible." Iri cleaned his plate, then placed his dishes in the wash bucket and gave them a swirl.

Beru chewed for a moment, then swallowed. "How much ground do you think we can cover?"

Iri looked resigned. "Not enough. We need more horses."

I rubbed my face, feeling defeated as he pointed out the main deficiency with our travel arrangements. "We don't have any more coin."

"With more horses, we could make better time."

I couldn't argue with that.

We'd taken turns walking next to the carriage or jostling around in the back of it. If we each had our own horse, the ride would be smoother and faster, and maybe I wouldn't ache so much at the end of the day. Maybe I wouldn't dreamwalk every night.

Something else was bothering me though, and I couldn't shake the strange restlessness I'd woken up with. Was it something from my dream, or my confusion about Beru? I didn't even realize I'd been jiggling my leg until Beru rested a hand on my knee.

"Are you okay?"

"Just want to get on the road." I leapt to my feet, dumping the rest of my drink on the fire.

"Astor hasn't eaten yet." Iri looked at me strangely.

I doubled down. "We have to get going. You know how he is. If we wait, it'll be midmorning before we go anywhere."

"She's right," Sade agreed, standing beside him. "He can eat on the road in the carriage if he can't get up with the rest of us. If we don't break camp now, it could be another hour or more until we get on the road."

Iri nodded, his face set in a surly expression that made him look even more dangerous than usual and retreated to the sleeping area. Beru followed, and together they woke the slugabed magician and began to pack up the sleeping pallets.

"Did you sleep okay? You seem off." She picked up the clean cookware, bundling it up before throwing it haphazardly into the back of the carriage.

"Okay enough." I didn't want to talk about the dreamwalking

now. I needed a break from everything, and particularly that. The moment had been lost earlier, and now after some distance I didn't want to bring it back.

She nodded and didn't push. We'd become good friends on our first adventure, and she knew me well enough to leave it alone when I answered in short sentences. Awkwardly, it made me want to tell her again.

"I just—" I stopped, unsure of what to say. I needed to tell someone, and she was my best option for honest advice with a side of discretion.

"If something is wrong, just tell me. It's clearly not doing you any good carrying it all by yourself." She placed her hand on my arm, her eyes inviting me to trust her.

"I ain't the only one needing beauty sleep from the looks of you ladies."

We whirled to see Astor yawning as he staggered up behind us.

Clearly restraining the urge to smack him, she narrowed her eyes and nodded toward the food. "There's a plate for you in the carriage."

"Umm, guys? I don't think I ordered that." He took a few steps back, his hand shaking as he pointed to something behind the carriage.

We turned.

At first, I wondered if he was bothered by the amount of meat. Then I saw the long black legs approaching in sets of eight.

They crept toward us, some the size of a bird, a few as big as our horses. By mutual unspoken agreement, we started inching toward the fire, trying to get Iri and Beru's attention without letting the giant spiders out of our sight.

"This is a little outside my comfort zone." Astor stepped behind us, using Sade as a shield.

"Really? No kidding." I looked at Sade. "Have you ever…?"

"No." She never took her eyes off the nearest spiders.

I made eye contact with Beru as we reached the smoldering remains of the fire. The surprise on his face told me he'd never seen anything like it either.

"Keep coming toward the fire." Iri picked up several large sticks, stoking the fire with one, then handed the others out.

"Don't worry about that." Astor took the stick, brandishing it. "I'll be staying right beside it until they disappear. Which I'm hoping will be *any* second now."

"Aim for their heads. They'll protect themselves with their legs." Iri stepped around the fire, placing himself in front of it. He would be the first line of defense between us and the spiders, the fire the second.

"So, is it true their legs...?" Astor began, stopping to swallow hard, his eyes wide as he stared at a dog-sized one approaching Iri.

Iri ran toward the spider, calling out his reply even as he leapt. "Are poisonous? Yes. Don't let them strike you." Using the force of his body to shove his stick into its head, Iri dispatched it with one blow.

Astor hooted. "So that's all there is to it?"

I smiled at his instant confidence, hoping it would help us all get out of this in one piece. I wondered why he wasn't using magic, instead of brandishing his stick awkwardly, but chalked it up to lack of training. Before I could ask, Sade ran toward another spider which had snuck up behind Iri.

"Don't hesitate. Move!" She jumped and slammed her stick into it the same way Iri had.

Then the spiders seemed to speed up.

I copied Iri's battle strategy to claim the life of the smallest spider, which had scurried around the fire and was approaching us from the side. Dreamwalking had exhausted me and knew I was slower than usual. But I couldn't afford to mess up.

If the spiders were as deadly as Astor feared, we wouldn't get a second chance.

We fought silently, each of us leaping and eliminating approaching spiders while Astor stood pale-faced almost in the fire, occasionally lashing out when one came too close to him. As we executed them, their eerie screams pierced my soul, leaving me oddly cold.

As their numbers dwindled, I began to relax. Out of nowhere, the remaining spiders stopped advancing and dispersed into the trees. It as if someone had sounded a retreat only they could hear.

Iri looked toward the forest, his face set in grim lines. Without dropping his weapon, he turned to me. "Someone's testing us."

I stood still, recalling the dark voice from the prison. Was this the gift it had promised?

CHAPTER 10

I tried to convince myself the spiders were a consequence of being in a new land with new creatures, but after we left, I noticed Sade and Iri whispering as they walked behind the carriage.

I wondered if they thought the spider attack was more than that, but they didn't say anything to me, and I was too scared to ask. It was bad enough being attacked, but worse if it turned out those creatures had intentionally been looking for us.

Beru was taking his turn guiding the horse while Astor and I rode in the back to rest our feet.

Astor scanned the woods, sitting vigilantly instead of slumped over like usual. "You think those things are still out there?"

"Hard to say." I sat opposite him, rubbing the calluses on my burning heels. Long days of walking hadn't been kind to them.

"How long until we get there?" A bag shifted and fell with a thump causing him to whip around and check behind him as if he'd thought a spider was attacking.

I smiled sympathetically, pulling my sock and boot back on

with a wince. "A while yet. We're heading as far west as possible."

"Shouldn't you heal yourself?"

"I need to rest first. My energy is low, and I've got to keep as much as I can in case we need to fight again." I glanced back at Sade and Iri, who were still deep in conversation.

"I wonder what they're talking about." His eyes narrowed as he considered them.

"The trip, I imagine." I looked at what we had left for supplies. It was enough for maybe two or three days.

"We'd better get more," he followed my gaze.

"The next town. We can see about getting some horses too, if we can make enough money. My feet can't handle walking much longer and we've got a long way to go still."

"How far to the next town?" Astor called out to Beru.

"*Whoa!*" Beru pulled back on the reins, slowing the horse to a stop. "One more sitting and we should be there." He jumped off the carriage, making his way to the woods without another word.

"Should we stop him?" Astor stood, obviously debating on leaping from the back of the carriage.

"I don't think he wants to empty his bladder in front of us." I kept my back toward the trees, allowing him some privacy as I gave Astor a pointed look.

He had the grace to flush before following my example.

Sade came up to us, holding her hands out. "Break time! Pass me the cups."

I handed her the bag of cups.

She managed to fill two from the water barrel before it ran dry, then split them evenly into five before shooting me an apologetic look.

"We're out."

"You take mine."

"Everyone drinks." She gave me a look, handing me a partially filled cup.

I accepted, unwilling to start an argument when she got *that* look on her face.

Beru emerged from the woods looking refreshed. He nodded his thanks when Sade passed him a cup of water. He drank it in one gulp, then jumped back in the carriage seat.

"We need those horses." Iri wiped his mouth. "We can't travel all the way to the coast with one carriage and horse. We should be switching the horse on the carriage at least three times a day to keep it healthy. At this rate, it will drop dead long before we get there."

"Next town's not far." Beru called back to us.

"That's all fine, but we still have no money." Sade pointed out the unfortunate truth as she put the cups back in the bag.

A slow smile spread over Astor's face. "The local governor has more than he knows what to do with."

"And he's just going to hand his horses over to us." I crossed my arms, wondering if he'd lost his wits.

"We could borrow them and return them on the way back." Astor took some venison from his pocket and bit a piece off as he looked between us for our reactions.

I wrinkled my nose in disgust, ready to tell him how dumb he sounded when Iri jumped in.

"Let's try a more reasonable route first."

"What's more reasonable?" Sade shrugged.

I stared at her. Surely, she didn't think Astor's idea had merit.

"I'll figure it out by the time we get there. Let's push on."

Iri nodded to Beru, who whipped the horse.

It began to walk at a slow pace and Astor jumped off, exchanging places with Sade.

I groaned in pain.

She held her hands up. "You stay. Iri still wants to walk."

I looked out to see Iri teasing Astor by imitating his long strides and chuckled. When I looked back into the carriage, she was punching a sack into shape to use as a pillow. She closed her eyes, leaving me alone with only my thoughts for company.

Beru glanced back, occasionally making eye contact but not speaking.

We didn't bother to stop again until we reached town, luckily with daylight to spare.

Beru pulled into a corral on the main street, then hopped out to tie up the horse and carriage.

"So, what's the plan, big man?" Astor jumped in the carriage, leaning forward to include Beru in his question.

"We take bets," Iri replied, searching in his pack for something, before finally pulling out his last few coins. "Astor, you stay and keep an eye on our things."

Astor leaned back on his crossed arms, placing his hat over his eyes. "No problem, boss."

"You take bets." Iri passed the coins to Sade along with a piece of paper. "I'll set up a bare-knuckle fight."

"I'll fight." Beru stepped forward and volunteered.

Iri clapped him on the back and walked toward the center of the town with Sade following close behind.

"You sure you want to do that?" I tried to hide my concern, looking between him and Iri. Based on size alone, would Iri not be a better bet?

"I'll win." Beru gave me a half-smile, leaning over the side of the carriage to check out the suspicious sound coming from the floor.

Astor was already asleep and snoring loudly.

"You're pretty confident."

"Yup." He didn't look away from the snoring boy.

"I'm sure Iri would do it if you wanted to back out." I pulled the latch on the back of the carriage up, locking it.

"Nope."

I sat down on a shady bench next to our horse, watching as he took refuge from the heat behind the carriage. I couldn't help but wonder how he was able to turn his emotions off and on like that.

He was a completely different man from the one who'd lain beside me last night. This was the emotionless warrior, without a hint of caring for anything or anyone evident on his face.

The sun had already begun to set by the time Sade and Iri returned, and it was clear from their satisfied smiles they'd managed to secure a fight.

"How many bets?" I stood and walked toward them.

"Enough for two horses." She winced at my expression of dismay. "It's a start. More people will bet when the fight starts."

"It's not enough for Beru to fight for."

Iri banged on the carriage to wake up Astor, who jumped up and grabbed an empty bag to protect himself. Iri chuckled at his reaction. "They'd pay us *not* to see you fight," Iri joked.

"We got food as well." Sade pulled a small bag from behind her back.

We descended on the food ravenously, excited to have some variety for a change after the venison and grain.

"Where is the fight?" Beru stretched his arms, yawning contentedly.

"It's in an old barn at dusk." She pulled out the coins she'd collected for the bets and counted it, looking disappointed as she shifted in her seat. "Make that one horse."

"I don't think we should chance it." I got up, returning to the bench I'd sat on all afternoon. I didn't like the risk.

Beru followed, sitting down beside me. Our thighs touched slightly, even though there was plenty of room on the bench. "It's our only shot at getting the money we need."

I shifted, hoping it wasn't obvious I'd moved my leg away. "You're no good to us hurt."

"I'll be fine." He leaned closer, his arm hanging over the back of the bench, almost encircling me and moving his leg so our knees lightly bumped together. "You think Iri's a better fighter, don't you?"

I didn't want to argue with him. Iri *was* a better fighter, but I knew he could hold his own. "I just don't see the point of a fight if it barely gets us anything in return and you get hurt. We'd be in an even worse position." I inched away again, uncomfortable at his closeness.

"There's nothing else you want to say to me?" His eyes were intense, staring into my soul.

I didn't know what he wanted from me.

He'd been distant all day, and now I couldn't smell anything but his musk as he drowned out everything else.

There was plenty I could say. It was right at the tip of my tongue. "No."

Beru leaned an inch closer and I froze. What was he doing?

My breath caught and before I knew it, he pulled back.

His face resumed its normal emotionless expression and confused, I turned to look straight ahead, focusing on Sade like she was my life line.

"Over here." Iri waved us over, breaking the awkward silence.

"We may have a better idea." Astor was practically bursting with excitement.

"Better?" I said slowly, looking between the three of them.

Sade shrugged, gesturing for Astor to speak.

"I know where the governor keeps his coin!" Astor blurted.

"And? Where are you going with this?"

"He's rich," Sade added helpfully.

"I'm guessing he got that way by not sharing it willy-nilly. He probably doesn't dish it out." I crossed my arms, raising an eyebrow. I was willing to hear them out but so far, it wasn't much of a plan.

Astor beamed. "No, but you can dreamwalk without anyone seeing you."

Sighing, I closed my eyes and tried to focus. It wasn't the best environment, but the back of the carriage was the safest place for me to attempt to dreamwalk into the governor's house. I was terrified of ending up in the prison again. I couldn't tell my friends the real reason for my reluctance to try their plan, and therefore, I'd grudgingly agreed to go along with the hare-brained scheme.

"It's in his office behind the picture."

"Shhh, Astor! She needs complete silence, remember?" Sade pulled him back, narrowly keeping him from falling into the wagon.

I glared at him, then closed my eyes and tried my best to concentrate. It took more time to get into a deep sleep with everyone watching, but soon enough I was in the governor's house. I caught a glimpse of myself in a mirror I passed. I was not invisible, but I didn't attempt to be. It would use too much energy if I tried, and this needed to be a quick job.

The home was large, immaculate, with grand carvings and rich colors everywhere I looked. The walls were almost double the size of a normal house's walls, with rooms almost the size of our kitchen garden to the small fields back home. If I wasn't careful, I could easily get caught.

I heard voices approaching and ducked behind the swaths of fabric which passed for curtains. Positive my hiding spot hid me completely and hearing no shouts of alarm, I cautiously peeked out.

A well-dressed man dropped a kiss on a delicate woman's forehead before she turned to walk up a grand staircase. He turned, and I ducked back behind the fabric before he saw me.

Luckily, a young maid distracted him as she walked by.

She paused at the bottom of the staircase, giving him a flirtatious look.

He patted her bottom and she slapped him playfully on the chest.

To my shock, he pulled her forward and kissed her passionately. My cheeks heated as I wondered what it would be like to kiss Beru like that.

"Darling," a woman called from the door at the top of the stairs.

I realized the woman upstairs must be his wife by the way his eyes widened, and he looked around quickly. Watching silently he ushered the maid off to another room and I settled back into my hiding spot to wait.

I hoped he'd be quick, because from what Astor had explained about the house, I was pretty sure the room he'd hidden the maid in was the same room he kept his money.

"Yes, my dear?" He walked out of the room without the maid, looking relaxed.

"Are you coming to bed?" Her voice was sharp, clearly unhappy at having to wait.

"Right behind you, my love. I'm turning out the lights." The man walked back to the room and the lady at the top of the stairs retreated, shutting the door to what I assumed was the bedroom.

I watched as he came back out of the room, peering up at the now-dark upstairs.

Once he'd verified she wasn't present, he ushered the maid out. He kissed her again, then walked up the stairs as she slipped away into the darkness.

Now was my chance. I darted out from behind the curtain into the office. It was as grand as the rest of the house. The room was filled with dark wood furniture and the largest windows I had ever seen. The painting hiding the safe was exactly where Astor had said it would be.

I crept over to it, using only the light from the moon to

guide me. The painting was of a beautiful woman dressed in green silk, with hair the color of honey.

"You like it?" A male voice came from behind me.

I turned to see a man with a tall, thin build leaning against the door frame as he watched me. "Yes," I murmured, frightened I'd been made. Now I was trying to decide how to escape.

"This was my grandmother, in her younger years." He came to stand beside me and for a moment, we both admired the painting.

"It's stunning."

"She was a brilliant woman. I'm afraid I have but a faint echo of her elegance." He raised an eyebrow, inhaling from his pipe as he devoured me with his eyes.

Not knowing what else to do, I nodded and pretended to be captured by the painting.

"How is it you came to be here, milady?" He looked down, eyes roaming my face with a glittering hunger I found uncomfortable.

"The door was open, and I've always wanted to see the inside." I turned, looking down through lowered eyelashes the way I'd seen a neighbor girl do once when she'd tried to catch my brother's interest.

"Darling," the woman called, seemingly right outside the room.

"Would you excuse me for just one moment?" The man smiled, bowing to me before he turned to chase his wife.

Grabbing my chance, I quickly stepped toward the painting and pushed it aside. In the wall where Astor said it would be was a box. I opened it and took as much as I could carry.

CHAPTER 11

"Do you think he'll notice?" Sade turned to me from the back of her horse, looking amused once I'd finished telling my story.

"I doubt it. I took quite a few, but there were far too many for me to do much more than make a tiny dent in the pile. And even if he does notice, I don't think he'll suspect me." I smiled, thinking back on the adventure with amazement. Both that I'd gone through with it *and* managed to escape without repercussion.

Beru listened without commenting, his lips pressed firmly together.

I wondered if he was jealous I'd almost been propositioned by the man. Part of me wanted to know what he'd do, but another part of me just wanted to keep riding and thought I was crazy for pushing.

"He was handsome. But not my type." I watched Beru, looking for any indication of what he was thinking.

He glanced back, curiosity lighting his eyes. "What is your type?"

His question caught me off guard, and I stuttered. "Well,

umm, I don't know." I paused, trying to think of how to describe my type without describing him.

"Does that mean you've never dated?" He pulled the reins of his horse, slowing it down, getting in trot with mine.

My face was instantly on fire. Why hadn't I dated, again? I couldn't let him know that. I tried to gather my thoughts and searched frantically for a comeback.

"Her type is a man with two legs. What was your wife like?" Sade came to my rescue.

Not only did she interrupt the moment, but she caused Beru to spur the horse about a meter ahead even as he replied. "Blonde and very quiet."

His wife had been the opposite of me.

I wished I'd never tried to bait him by telling him about the man at the house.

Sade caught my eye, rolling hers. "You are his type," she mouthed.

I glanced at Beru, but he was farther ahead now.

"We got what we needed. That's what's important," Sade reminded me as we settled into an even trot beside each other.

"And my spell worked. The coin was exactly where I'd envisioned." Astor sat tall in his saddle. He'd been smiling proudly ever since I returned with all the coin we'd needed.

"Exactly where you said. Except you forgot the part about how handsy he is." I laughed, thinking of the governor and his many probable mistresses.

"That was a surprise." Astor waved his fingers in the air. "It wouldn't have changed anything though."

"I pity his dear wife." That poor woman must have known how friendly her husband was. Yet for some unknown reason, she tolerated it.

"She's got all the coin she could ever want." She brought her horse closer.

I shook my head. "I could never have a husband like that, no matter how much coin he had." I caught Beru turning his head slightly to listen to our conversation.

She snorted, shaking with withheld laughter. "Wouldn't bother me none."

I didn't doubt she meant what she said. She was fiercely independent and used to being on her own until I'd convinced her to join me in my quest to save Gavin. I wondered if she'd ever been in love. Surely, that would change how she felt about sharing.

Screams from the other side of the hill interrupted my thoughts.

We urged our horses to the top of the hill ahead for a better vantage point.

"Spiders," Iri said, reaching the top of the hill first.

"How many?" Sade was a close second.

"More than we encountered at the camp." Iri did his best to steady his horse as it began to dance beneath the reins, nervous at the sight of the spiders.

I rounded the hill with my horse to see at least sixty spiders in the process of attacking a small village. A few bodies lay across the ground, unmoving.

One of the spiders was using its tarsal claws as daggers while it held a victim with its pedipalp. That was where the screaming was coming from.

"Aria and I will fight the spiders. Iri and Sade, get as many people away from the village as you can. Astor…" Beru paused, brow furrowed as he looked at the youth. "Help the villagers."

Astor's face was pale, but he set his jaw and followed Iri and Sade without complaint.

I followed Beru's lead, galloping down the hill toward the village. As we neared the battle, thoughts raced through my head.

The villagers were no match for the spiders, and unless we

were as deadly and quick, more bodies would join those we could already see.

Scanning the field, I noticed a single ur'gel in the middle of the fray. It was a female, with the legs and body of a spider but the upper body of a woman wearing an iridescent black breastplate. Her face was oddly beautiful in a cruel, inhuman way, as if cut from marble, with glittering black eyes placed in the middle as if for decoration.

She was steady, without any sign of hesitation as they fought the villagers mercilessly, instructing the spiders to attack everyone, including the women and children. The other spiders surrounded her protectively as they followed her every command.

I glanced at Beru, and I knew we were thinking the same thing as his eyes narrowed. In unison, we changed directions.

As we headed straight toward her, a sickening smile spread over her face.

My horse whinnied, shying away from moving any closer when we were about ten feet from the spiders, so I jumped off a split second after him.

Both horses instantly ran back up the hill. Clearly, they were smarter than us.

We remained where we'd dismounted, sizing up the situation as the smaller spiders fought all around us, effectively trapping us in a ring. The ur'gel-spider-woman skittered across the ground, lessening the space between us as the other spiders moved back to allow her through.

At the last moment, she leapt, landing a mere foot away. "I've waited for this day for quite some time." Her words came out in a hollowed hiss, and faster than my eye could follow, she flung Beru to the side with one powerful front leg.

I stepped back, unsheathing my sword, and brandishing it in front of me. I swung only once before another leg yanked it out of my hands as easily as plucking a flower.

She moved toward me; her smile replaced by a frown at my attempt to fight her.

A long, barbed, black tongue spiraled out of her mouth and flicked back and forth as her eyes flashed from black to white.

My attempt at fighting her had merely angered her. I glanced at Beru for help, but he was still flat on the ground, unmoving. From the corner of my eye, I could see Sade and Iri holding back the other spiders as Astor guided a handful of villagers up the hill toward our carriage. I needed to buy them time somehow.

I grabbed the small knife from my hip. With my sword out of my reach, it was all I had, but useless unless I got closer. Maybe I could bluff my way out of this. "You need to leave these people alone."

A roar of laughter left her body, the noise a deafening, high-pitched screech.

I fought the urge to cover my ears, not wanting to show weakness.

One of her legs shot out, but I was quicker.

Jumping back, I sliced at her patella, missing. If I had to cut off each leg, one at a time, I'd do it. I just had to make contact.

Behind her, Iri was dragging Beru up the hill toward the carriage. Relief filled me until she saw where my gaze had gone.

"Loverboy will be fine," she cooed maliciously, swiping at me again.

I lifted my knife and tried to injure her leg, but once again I wasn't quick enough.

She laughed even harder at my attempt, advancing as I backed away. "Ooooh, is this a touchy subject, little dreamwalker?"

"How do you know what I am?" My face flushed at the thought of her knowing something so intimate about me. I refused to let her distract me from the legs which were reaching toward me.

"Do you not know who I am?" Her face was now only a few inches away from mine, her long hair brushing my cheek. As she crooned the words almost lovingly into my ear, her halitosis infused breath turned my stomach. I couldn't move, trapped in her glittering eyes.

"Run!" Iri screamed as he swung his sword, cutting one of her legs from its socket.

The shriek she emitted was soul-shattering, and enough to break the spell she'd had me under. She whipped around, focusing her attention on him while Sade yelled for me to run again.

My legs felt stupid and numb, and I watched as she stabbed at Iri with her remaining tarsi, one after another. For a while he managed to dodge them, but he couldn't keep it up forever.

With that thought powering me, I was able to break free and run toward Sade. I looked over my shoulder, seeing the ur'gel-spider snap her head in a complete one-eighty then reverse course, using her remaining seven legs to leap at me. I turned to run up the hill just in time to catch the sword Sade threw at me.

I stopped running and turned to face the spider.

She kept her distance this time, the other spiders standing with her again, lined up behind her. Every set of eyes now focused on me.

She let out a hiss, snapping her fingers. The sea of spiders parted, and one large spider brought Iri forward, dropping him at the feet of their leader. He was wrapped in a web, unable to move, yet awake and furious.

I hadn't noticed Sade at my side until she spoke, her voice hushed with awe. "I can't believe I'm seeing this."

"What?" I was annoyed at her reaction.

She should be trying to figure out how to get us out of this mess instead of sounding impressed.

"It's Widow." She stood looking at the creature in awe.

The spider glided across the grass, stopping a safe distance from the reach of my sword. "Finally, someone who knows me." She ran her hand through her long hair, shaking it off her face dramatically before giving me a disappointed look. "You know, you aren't that bright for a dreamwalker. I expected a little better from you." She pouted, examining the sharp, black nails on her humanoid front hands.

I started forward in anger, but Sade grabbed my arm and held me back, shooting me a warning look. "Don't let her get to you."

"Oh, I'm sorry. Did I hurt your little feelings?" Widow stuck her lip out, pouting, then cocked her head. To my surprise, her neck extended until her head was above us without moving the rest of her body at all. "You poor little thing. I know what would make you feel better. I'll give you back your friend." She motioned to Iri, who mumbled something under the webs holding his mouth shut.

Based on the fury in his eyes, I could only imagine it wasn't polite.

Widow's eyes narrowed, and she swung her head down to lick his cheek. The webs surrounding his face broke as he screamed in pain.

"She's baiting us. Don't." It was my turn to hold Sade back.

Apparently tired of Iri, Widow turned her attention back to us. She crept forward, her spiders inching along with her.

I glanced toward the hill, seeing Astor struggling to get Beru into the carriage.

He was still unconscious. This was not going well.

When I turned back, Widow was closer. With a smile wider than any I'd seen, she taunted us, her front hands making a "come-hither" gesture. Before I could think to stop her, Sade lunged forward with her sword held high and swinging.

Widow lashed out. I heard a loud "clunk" when her leg hit Sade, knocking her off her feet and flinging her several feet out of the circle of spiders.

Now it was just Widow and me.

"I expected more. This was disappointingly easy, like taking an afternoon walk. It's always such a letdown when you expect greatness and receive fly soup instead." Her black tongue licked at her lips as she sauntered closer.

I tried to step back, but one of her legs reached out, wrapping around my waist. I struggled to break free, but she held me effortlessly with the sticky appendage.

She yawned, lifting me above her head and dangled me, turning me from side to side. She was enjoying my fear even as I tried to suppress my tears.

"Do you know why I'm here?" Widow waited for me to respond, giving me a little shake when I took too long.

"No." Obviously, she was here to kill me.

"The God of Darkness sends his love. I'm Dag'draath's gift." She flung her head back and laughed, the noise compounding the headache I already had from her shrieks.

I looked at Astor, the only one of my friends still awake and squinted when I watched his mouth moving. Was he telling me to dreamwalk? I glanced at Widow. I didn't know if I could do it, but I had no other options. Closing my eyes, I prayed to all the gods I could think of. I had to somehow transport my body and hope I could bring her with me. It was clear I was the one she wanted, and the reason for the spider attacks.

Dag'draath had sent her for me, just as he'd promised he would.

I'd dreamwalked under pressure before, but never with my body. I quested down to the ground, searching for the energy and using the magic of Lynia herself. I prayed she'd be generous as I shut every noise out of my mind. I felt Widow's anger grow as her grip tightened on me.

I opened my eyes, expecting to still be trapped in her grip, but instead, I appeared to be in the dreamplane, a place between Lynia and dreamwalking. I felt my body, and it was whole as I stood with ease. Fear ran off my body like rain as all the negative emotions disappeared. I felt calm for the first time in a long time in the pure white room, free from danger.

I wanted to stay, relishing the unexpected moment of freedom. I had no idea how much time had passed though and knew I needed to return to my friends and heal them. The longer I waited, well, I wouldn't think about that.

I closed my eyes and prepared to go back. After several moments where bright light shone on my eyelids, I knew it hadn't worked. I refocused and tried again. It was harder without access to Lynia and her energy, because now I had to rely completely on my own power.

The memory of lying next to Beru after dreamwalking to the prison filled me. The warmth of his body near me, the comfort I'd felt. Darkness fell and I opened my eyes.

I could feel Lynia underneath me as I slowly sat up, the pain from my fall making my movements slow and stiff. I was back where I'd been before trying to dreamwalk, but now Widow and her spiders were gone.

Sade was on the ground beside me, unmoving.

Silence filled the clearing.

CHAPTER 12

"I can't do this anymore." Sade turned away, shaking her head as she stood up.

I'd spent the last two days healing Astor, Beru, and Sade, and I was too drained to get up and follow her. Iri was weak but on the mend and we were waiting for a local healer to arrive to finish his healing. He would have been there sooner, but the surviving villagers had needed him more than we did.

"I know it's been a lot." Panic set in. I couldn't go on without her. She was my rock and soldier, and I needed her guidance.

"I don't need this kind of trouble in my life." Sade had begun to pace, agitation present in every step she took across the floor.

I stood up to close the door, my legs shaking as if I was walking uphill. I had to fix this, but it needed to be done in private. "I get it. It's hard. But we couldn't have gotten as far as we have without you. I would have been dead so many times already."

"This is going to end in death."

Sade stopped at the window, standing with her back to me, every muscle tense as she pretended to look out of the dirty glass.

"I need you. I'm not going to lie and say I don't. I've learned so much from you, but there's so much more I need to know."

"Did you tell Beru?" She half-turned, looking at me with narrowed eyes as she waited.

"Tell him what?" I squinted, confused as to what she was asking.

"Did you tell him you've been going back to the prison? Since you've rescued him?" Her eyes bored into me.

I had to look away. I couldn't tell if she was angry or jealous, but I was ashamed I'd kept it to myself when it was because of me everyone had been injured. "I didn't tell anyone," I admitted in a whisper, unable to meet her gaze.

"Well, you certainly didn't tell me." She turned back to the window, crossing her arms.

"I'm sorry. I wanted to figure this out myself first. I was wrong."

"So much for needing me." She barely spoke loud enough for me to hear, but it compounded my guilt, nonetheless.

"I should have told you." I lowered my head, clasping and unclasping my hands. I had the same feeling in the pit of my stomach I'd gotten when my brother told me to leave. For a moment, I wondered if I needed to empty my stomach. I was scared I would, and choked the bile back.

We'd grown as close as family and I couldn't handle another abandonment.

"But you didn't." Sade's voice wavered, and for a moment, I wondered if she was holding back tears.

I stepped closer, but when she stiffened, I changed my mind about approaching her. I hung back, unsure whether to stand or sit. I knew I had to convince her to stay with me. She was a pivotal part of the team and my life.

"I can fix this. I know I can." But how? I couldn't find the words I needed.

"I need some time. I'll have to think about it." She turned her head to the side, still avoiding eye contact. "I'd like to be alone."

"Okay."

I walked slowly toward the door, hoping she would turn and tell me she'd been joking. But when I reached it without any movement, I sighed, and left to check on the others, closing the door gently behind me.

"Is she okay?" Astor was on his way to the room, and I grabbed his wrist just as he reached for the handle.

I tried to smile, but it fell flat. "She asked to be alone."

"What's wrong?" He turned his head to the door, then looked at me with a frown.

"I can't talk about it," I managed to choke out, then took off down the hall as hot tears escaped to run freely down my cheeks. With my vision blurred, I bumped into something hard and looked up, startled to see Beru looking down at me.

"What's wrong?"

I pushed him away and ran out of the house. I didn't want Sade to see me talking to him and couldn't handle explaining my feelings to him of all people.

Once I was sure no one had followed me, I sat on the ground with my back to a tree and sobbed into my hands. How had everything changed so much? I'd lost so much this year. I barely recognized myself.

I hated I'd let Beru come between us. Ever since I'd dreamwalked him out of prison I'd been unable to get him out of my head. I was putting others at risk for him. I swore I wouldn't do that again. I'd never be alone with him again, no matter what.

Burying my head in my arms, I cried until I couldn't cry anymore. Once my tears dried up, I sat numb to the world, the bright sun on my back mocking me with its cheeriness.

"Aria!" Someone was calling me from the house.

I ignored it, then they called again. It was Beru. I hunched over, trying to make myself smaller. Maybe the large tree stump would hide me from him. I wasn't strong enough to resist him. I needed more time if I was going to uphold my promise to myself.

"Aria?" He came closer. "I can see you there."

I sighed loudly, making certain he could hear me.

"It's Iri." He approached slowly.

I jumped up my inner turmoil forgotten as I recognized his solemn expression. "What's wrong?"

"He's worse. Much worse."

Guilt flooded me again. I'd tended to Beru before Sade, before Iri. And now Iri was failing. My face reddened with shame at how I'd let him interfere with my decisions. I ran past him to the house as fast as my legs would carry me. All that mattered was getting to Iri.

I pushed the door open, finding Astor and Sade already by the bedside.

She was crying softly as Astor attempted to soothe her. "Where were you? We looked everywhere." Sade stood up, her face red.

I saw judgment in her eyes and shifted my gaze to Iri. I couldn't deal with her right now, so I bent down instead of replying. I blocked my turbulent emotions as best as I could and examined my patient.

Iri was drenched in sweat. I felt for his heart rate. Too slow. My pulse picked up, and I began to question my abilities. I was in way over my head and my energy was too low to chance draining myself completely. "When is the local healer arriving?"

"He should have been here by now." Beru brought a chair to the head of the bed, straddling it as he sat, leaning his arms on the top of the back as he looked down on Iri.

"We sent someone to find him just before you returned," Astor added helpfully.

I looked at Sade, who was kneeling on the floor beside the bed.

She hadn't let go of his hand.

I lowered myself to sit at the opposite end of the bed, but she avoided looking at me. I held back my tears at the loss of my friend and focused on being there for Iri in the best way I could.

Seeing no other options, I placed my hands over Iri and focused what little energy I had on him.

Astor saw what I was doing and placed his hand on my shoulder.

I turned to him, and he nodded, a half-smile on his face. I smiled back, then closed my eyes, and carefully tapped into his energy.

It was a dangerous gamble, as I had no way of knowing how much energy I could take.

He was still healing from the attacks himself, and if I took too much it would undo my previous work.

We sat in silence as I harnessed as much energy as I could.

Astor stepped aside as Beru took his place, then Sade.

My hands began to shake, but I held on for as long as my friends were willing to give their energy. I leaned over, so I didn't have to hold myself up. I could give that to Iri as well. Soon, my eyes wanted to close. I fought to keep them open, lasting until dusk before I finally had to stop.

I couldn't lift myself off the floor.

Beru picked me up, even though he was still weak himself. He sat me in a nearby chair and Astor wrapped me in a blanket, handing me warm tea as shivers wracked my body.

"How is he?" Astor sat in the chair beside me.

"I don't know. I don't know what's wrong with him. He's stronger for the moment, but everything I give him keeps depleting so fast. I've never seen anything like it." I shook my head, not knowing what to do next.

We all sacrificed everything we had to spare of our own energy, and it still wasn't enough.

The door flew open and a stranger entered the room, filling it with the cool night air. "Where is he?"

"Over here." Beru called him over to the bed.

The man's eyebrows shot up. He strode over, dropping his medicine bag on the floor beside the bed and began his examination. "When did this happen?"

"Two days ago, when we were fighting off spiders," Astor told him as he placed a large pot of boiling water on the table beside the bed.

"Did she bite him?" The healer examined Iri for wounds, turning swiftly to me.

"Bite him?" I stood up, my legs trembling slightly as I walked over to the bed.

"Yes. Bite." He made an exaggerated biting movement with his mouth, looking at each of us in turn.

"She licked him. Widow, I mean."

When they all stared at me, I realized I must have been the only one awake to witness it.

"He's poisoned." The healer nodded once, digging through his bag.

"Poisoned?" Sade sniffled, fresh tears springing to her eyes.

"Her fangs are poisonous. None of you knew?" He shook his head, then placed his ear over Iri's chest, holding up one hand to quiet the room. "Hmm, he's pretty far gone."

"Can you help?" Terror filled me at the idea I would lose another of my friends. It was all my fault. I couldn't live with myself if he died.

"I'll know in the morning. Right now, I need a table."

Beru slid a second table over to the bed as the healer unpacked his bag.

With the hot water on the other table and ingredients from his bag he began measuring and mixing powders together.

At first, I just watched, but after a few moments I approached. Maybe I could help.

"You were a healer." He didn't turn to look at me, continuing to work as he waited for a reply.

"Yes. Not a very good one though."

"Good enough. He'd be dead otherwise." He glanced at me, smiling briefly before looking back at his work.

"What are you doing?" I marveled at everything he had contained in the bag. The ingredients were more numerous than I'd expected once outside their container.

"I'm making two different plasters to draw out the poison. Once they've done all they can, we will offer him more energy to restore his life force."

He handed me the first paste in a small mortar, gesturing for me to take it to the bedside, then swiftly grabbed another and ground different herbs, mixing them as well. He joined me a moment later, passing me the next mortar. I placed it with the first bowl on the bed beside Iri and waited as he washed his hands in the remainder of the hot water.

"Where did she lick him?" He held out a hand for the first bowl.

I passed it to him, pointing out the discolored patch on Iri's face. "His left cheek."

He quickly slathered the paste on the skin with the bruising. "The most minuscule amount of her saliva in an open wound can be deadly."

He concentrated, his hands steady and wise as he focused solely on Iri's still form. He repeated the process with the second paste, and tears sprang to my eyes at the thought of Mother Ofburg. His movements were so similar the memory stung.

"Now, we wait." He reached over, patting my shoulder.

I wiped away my tears, blinking rapidly to avoid breaking down, and watched Iri as the healer got up and began to tidy his supplies. I hoped this would work, otherwise tomorrow we may need to bury him.

"He won't heal in front of your eyes." He glanced at me reprovingly.

I turned away, embarrassed at being caught. "I know."

I stood up, emotionally and physically drained. My friends were all asleep by the fire, sleeping innocently after expending their energy to help.

"Here." He passed me a clean bowl, waving toward the prep table. "You're up next."

"Oh, no. You have to do it." I pushed it back.

He stepped forward, firmly placing it in my hand and wrapping the other around the bowl. "It's your turn. You can use any of my supplies. I think you'll feel better if you do this." Gently, he pushed me toward the table and brought a chair for me. When I sat down, he clapped my shoulder in approval. "I'll rest while I wait for this to take effect. Wake me when you're finished."

I nodded, still unsure I should be interfering, but he joined the others on the floor, covering up with a blanket and closed his eyes, leaving me alone with my doubts.

I closed my eyes, listening to the memory of Mother Ofburg's voice and allowing her to guide my movements. Working quickly with my eyes closed, I reached into my pocket and pulled out a few weeds from her garden, adding them for good measure.

When I opened my eyes, the paste almost seemed to glow in the dark. I moved to the side to look at it under the light, and it sparkled as the fire hit it.

"It's time to try your ointment."

I whirled around, startled to see him standing behind me. I exhaled shakily, handing the new paste to him with a smile. "It's ready."

I wiped the old paste from Iri's face, revealing raw, red skin beneath it. He passed my paste over, and I gently coated the area. As I finished, Iri began to moan, restlessly tossing his head from side to side.

I glanced up at the healer, who simply nodded. "I must go. I can see he's in good hands."

"You can't leave." I stood up quickly. I couldn't be trusted with his life.

"It was you who healed him, not I." The healer held his hands over Iri for a moment, then let them drop, a look of satisfaction on his face. "You'll know for certain in the morning. But he's turned a corner now."

"But what if he worsens?" I felt lightheaded as my heart pumped faster, anxiety setting in. I couldn't bear if anything happened on my watch.

"Make another batch of your paste. Wait till it dries, then reapply it. Do that every two hours." He packed up his belongings, leaving out the herbs I'd made my paste from, along with the mortar and pestle. "I'll be back in the morning for what's left."

I didn't argue as I watched him leave, even though I wanted to protest I shouldn't be trusted. Once he was gone, I turned back to the bed. I wondered if it was just my imagination when it seemed as if his breathing had smoothed out. I turned to look at Sade, sleeping peacefully with the others.

I prayed when morning arrived, everything would be okay again.

CHAPTER 13

I hated small spaces. I held my breath and crawled inside the small cabinet anyway. Breathing as shallowly as possible, I prayed I could be anywhere but here.

"That's no way to greet an old friend." Dag'draath's voice seemed to reverberate through my bones. "Aria come out and play," he purred, drawing out the word play in a strange singsong fashion which was at odds with the harshness of his voice.

I pinched myself. Hard. "Wake up!" I knew I'd slipped into dreamwalking and into the prison again, and it was the last place I wanted to be.

"Little dreamwalker, come out and play." His voice was closer, teasing me. "Where have you run to, little mouse?"

I cracked the cabinet door just enough to see a shadow move beneath the closed door to the room, then pause. I could feel him standing there, waiting. Calling for me to come to him. I closed the cabinet door and pinched myself again.

There had to be a reason I kept returning. Think. A connection of some sort. I opened the cabinet again, and this time his shadow was gone. I jumped out, knowing I couldn't stay in one spot for long. I needed a place to lie down so I could focus on dreamwalking my scrawny self out of the prison for good, but I also needed to figure out how not to come back.

I remembered where I found Beru. He used to hide to be alone. If I could get to one of his hiding spots, I could relax. I slowly crept to the door, trying to be as silent as possible. I pressed my ear to the door, listening for Dag'draath. When it remained silent, I reached for the handle, praying he'd moved on to search another room.

A loud click echoed off the walls and I cringed. It sounded like thunder in the quiet and I debated whether to turn it further. I did not want to draw his attention if he had moved past me. I stood completely still as I waited to hear his horrible voice bellowing through the hallway.

When I heard nothing after what felt like an eternity, I decided it was as safe as it would ever be. I turned the knob the rest of the way, pulling the door an inch toward me. Light spilled into the room. The hallway was clear from where I stood, but I had a fifty-fifty chance he was behind the door.

When my impatience outweighed my fear, I decided to make a break for it. I couldn't wait forever, and one way or another I'd have to deal with the consequences. Swinging the door all the way open before I could change my mind, I darted into the hallway. I turned full circle, hands up to fight if needed.

The hallway was empty.

I took a deep breath and ran toward the closest hiding place I remembered, trying to keep my steps light without slowing down. When I came to an open door, I flattened myself against the wall and listened.

Nothing.

Now or never. I craned my neck to look inside, darting back when I saw two men. Luckily, they were reading a map on the wall and didn't notice me. I made a mental note to return to look at the map if I had a chance, then continued.

I knew I was close. It was only one more turn, then four

more doors to his hiding place. When I approached the corner my heart rate kicked up a notch. I listened for noise, and when I heard nothing, I stuck my head around it, just enough to survey the hall.

All clear.

I turned the corner, breathing easier since I only had four doors to go. I could make it. I crept down the hall, remaining as close to the wall as I could. The first two doors were closed, but the third was open and voices rose loudly from inside. I couldn't understand what they were saying, but laughter spilled out.

I peeked inside. Three men. One facing the door, two facing away. I could probably slip by unnoticed. I looked behind me to make sure it was still clear. Voices came from the other end of the hallway now. My time was up. I needed to move immediately, so I darted across the door, praying to reach my destination.

"Hey! A girl just ran by!"

I reached for the doorknob of the safe room, panicking when I found it locked. I pulled harder, looking over my shoulder. I expected all three men to be staring at me, but no one had found me yet. I turned the knob the other direction, and by the grace of Yina'ane'ut it swung open. I pushed inside and closed the door, locking it behind me.

By now the men had caught up and I could hear them searching. The doorknob rattled as someone tried it.

I was too scared to breathe, so I closed my eyes and willed myself into a statue, holding my breath until I couldn't any longer. When I finally chanced it, I heard them move past the door down the hallway. After a few minutes longer, their voices became distant and disappeared.

I walked to the other side of the room, where a small, dirty window in the corner allowed a sliver of light to enter the room. From the faint glow, I was able to make out the cot I'd seen Beru take refuge on in the past. I lay down on the cot gratefully, catching a hint of his scent.

Pushing it out of my mind, I tried to get comfortable and focus. I needed to get out of this dream. I closed my eyes, resting my hands by my sides.

The room filled with light, and I sat up abruptly. Light streamed in from beneath the door as the knob jiggled. Then the door slammed, almost buckling under the weight of someone attempting to force it open with their body.

"Aria, where are your manners?" It was Dag'draath. He was right outside the door.

Forcing myself to lie down and close my eyes, I began chanting a refrain, hoping to wake up in my own bed. The door banged and cracked, threatening to open as I pressed my eyes closed more tightly.

"*Wake up.*" Someone was calling me faintly, but it wasn't here. It was someone on the other side, trying to wake me up.

I focused on their voice, scrambling to latch on and climb it like a rope.

The door gave way, flying off its hinges and across the room, narrowly missing me.

I lost my breath.

There was no air.

I sat up, frantically scratching at my throat until I saw Beru was the one shaking me.

"Wake up! Are you all right?" He had both of my shoulders in his hands and looked terrified.

"Umm, yes. Thank you." I sucked as much air as possible into my lungs, feeling my panic slowly subside. As it did, I realized I was in one of the bedrooms. I moved away from him as awkwardness pushed aside the residual fear.

"You were in the prison?" He stepped around the bed, blocking my retreat.

I didn't answer him. I couldn't. Brushing him past with one

hand on the wall to steady myself, I headed for the door and hoped he wouldn't follow. I had to check on Iri. I didn't know how long I'd been asleep.

Beru was quicker, moving in front of me again. "Why would you risk going back there?"

"Do you really think I wanted to go back there? I didn't decide to go back there. I don't get to decide where I go when I slip into a dreamwalk when I'm already asleep." I was annoyed, partly at his arrogance, but also because I needed distance from him. I was thankful he'd woken me when he had, but I didn't want him to know what had almost happened.

He reached out his arm as I tried to push past him. Somehow, I ended up in the nook between his arm and chest, and his body half-surrounded me. "If I have to wake up fifteen times a night to keep you here, I will."

I stared into his eyes and for a moment, I wanted to stay.

He bent his head slightly, his face far too close for comfort, and as his eyes drifted half-closed.

I did the only thing that came to mind—I ducked.

He lost his balance and I was free to leave. "We still need to discuss this."

I walked away rapidly, wincing as he called after me, and made my way to the main room where we'd been taking turns watching Iri. I half-expected, half-hoped he'd follow me, but he didn't. My heart sank even as I mentally smacked myself on the back of the head. I needed to decide what I wanted, or I was going to drive myself to distraction.

I couldn't deny our connection, and it seemed he felt the same. As time went on, we were becoming closer, but I needed to keep my distance. I still barely knew anything about him, or if I could trust his reason for being in the prison in the first place.

I found myself drifting back to the various moments we'd been alone.

We seemed to understand each other so well.

I felt so connected to him I sometimes wondered if I could speak to him by thought alone. If I could, I was far too scared to try. I couldn't feel so strongly about someone who was evil, could I.

I leaned against the post, closing my eyes as I tried to push him from my mind. A moment later, I opened them and entered the main room to find Iri sitting up in bed eating breakfast as Sade fussed over him.

They hadn't noticed me standing there, and to my surprise, it looked like Sade was flirting with him while he ate it, and the food she was feeding him, up.

He looked over, spotting me as she hand-fed him a strawberry. His face flushed and he pushed her hand away. "Aria."

She stood without looking at me and walked out the front door.

I sat next to him on the bed, reaching my hand out to feel his pulse. I exhaled when I felt it, strong and regular. "It was touch and go last night."

"You saved me. Sade told me it was your medicine that saved me." He smiled, eyes sparkling with gratitude.

I brushed his comment off. After what he'd been through, I didn't deserve any thanks. "How are you feeling today?"

"Not ready to stand yet but getting there." He returned to his food, eating as if he was starving. I imagined he was, since he hadn't eaten much in the last three days.

"Did she talk to you ... about me?" I nodded toward the front door, unsure whether I should have even asked but unable to help myself.

"She loves you. Go talk to her."

Was that really a good idea? She already wasn't sure she wanted to continue our journey with what had happened, and I worried anything I said would make things worse. I could handle anyone else hating me but her.

"Go," he ordered, pushing me away from the bed.

I got up, dragging my feet as I headed to the door. I saw her sitting by the water's edge and made my way over to her. What could I say to convince her to come with me? To risk her life for me. She risked her life most days, but it was for causes she believed in. Maybe she didn't believe in me anymore.

I stopped, standing beside her. I hadn't come up with anything brilliant, and she didn't acknowledge I was even there. I cleared my throat. "Well, Iri seems to be in better spirits."

"He's alive." She leaned over to pick up a rock, throwing it across the top of the water, watching it skip seven times before finally dropping beneath the surface.

"I don't know where we went wrong, but you have no idea how important you are to me. I don't want to go through life without you." I spit it all out, saying everything I could think of to make her understand how much I needed her.

She turned her head, raising an eyebrow. "Stop begging already. I'm coming with you."

My jaw dropped. "Really? When did you change your mind?" The second I asked I wished I hadn't. I didn't want her to reconsider.

She skipped another rock, shrugging. "I don't want to go back to being alone."

"I'll never let that happen, I promise." The thought of her being alone made me teary and I leaned in, needing a hug. I was prepared to face her rejection, but she squeezed back tightly, if somewhat awkwardly, for a moment before pulling away.

"Okay, I'm done." Smiling, I sat looking at the water. Right then, everything was perfect, and I had my best friend back.

"When should we leave?" She threw another rock but it only skipped once.

"Tomorrow. Iri should be strong enough to last a few hours in the back of the carriage by then." I debated asking her about the moment I'd interrupted but didn't want to test my luck.

"Thank you. For saving him." She evaded my gaze, as if searching for the perfect rock was the most important job she had at that moment.

"I'd have done it for any of you."

"I'm sorry for what I said about Beru. I know you two have a thing. I was mad and I shouldn't have said what I did." She wrinkled her nose as she looked up.

"Did you really think I'd pick him over you?"

"Someday you will, Aria. But that's okay." She gave me a sad half-smile, then returned to skipping rocks.

"Aria! Sade!" Beru called from the house, waving us back.

"We're having a girl moment!" She yelled back at him.

"It will have to wait. We've got bigger problems."

CHAPTER 14

"So, she's just attacking everyone?" I wiped the sweat off my forehead as I paced between the fireplace and the front door.

"She wants us to come to her." She sat beside Iri, watching me with a stoic expression.

"None of us are ready to fight right now." Iri pulled himself into a sitting position with some difficulty.

I wasn't certain if he'd done it intentionally, but the sight of such a powerful warrior struggling to sit up shook my confidence to the core.

"People are dying. She shows no mercy to anyone. Women and children are fair game to her." Beru shook his head, taking a sip from his cup.

I noticed he'd been avoiding me since I'd returned with Sade, speaking only to the others, or if he had to speak to me, as part of the group. I'd guess I'd finally pushed him away too many times. I couldn't blame him. I averted my eyes and tried to only focus on the problem at hand.

I stopped in the middle of the room as a plan began to

percolate. "We have to give her what she wants, but not how she expects to get it."

"How do we do that?" Astor spoke from the corner. He'd been so quiet I'd forgotten he was there.

"I'm not sure yet," I wasn't back to a hundred percent yet. My thoughts were still slow, and I was frustrated by my memory lapses. Between dreamwalking the night before and all the healing I'd done, I still had very little energy.

"We can't play her game." Beru stood up, addressing everyone else without looking at me again.

This time, I didn't hide my annoyance. It wasn't some petty him against me game, but it seemed to me anything I said, he wanted the opposite. I saw Sade's eyes sharpen as she looked between us, and I could tell she felt something was wrong.

"I don't think that's what Aria meant."

Beru glanced at me for the first time since he'd called us back. His lips were a firm white line. Without notice, he walked to the front door and stormed out.

"What's that all about?" She gestured toward where he had just stood.

"He's mad because I wouldn't talk to him." I tried my best to downplay the earlier moment.

"I'd think he'd be happy." Sade smiled, cocking an eyebrow.

I knew I'd be grilled for details when we were alone but I wanted to focus on what was important. "It's not what you think. Let's get back to what we're going to do next."

"I'd like to discuss this now." She grinned, but Iri shifted on the bed, clearly uncomfortable with where the conversation was headed.

"I knew it!" Astor walked over to the bed to join us. "There *is* something going on between you."

"*Whoa*! We are not discussing this. Not now, not ever." I held up my hands and backed away from them. I didn't know how I felt about Beru, but I certainly wasn't about to discuss it with everyone until I did.

"We'll discuss Widow only. Your personal life is your own." Iri tried to regain control of the conversation.

Thankful for his efforts, I agreed and sat down in the chair Beru had vacated. "Widow is all I want to talk about."

"Astor, get Beru to come back please." Iri pointed his chin at the door, and Astor nodded and left.

"How are you feeling now? Any better?" I leaned over, placing the back of my hand on his forehead as I checked for any sign of fever.

"I'll be fine." He leaned closer, whispering. "I'm rather enjoying being pampered." He glanced at Sade, who was refilling his glass as he spoke. They were complete opposites, but I hoped they could both let their guards down to the possibility of each other.

"So, how do we beat Widow and her army?" She forced him to drink his water then took a seat on a chair next to him.

Astor came in the front door with a stupid grin on his face, a scowling Beru following a few steps behind.

I wondered what Beru had told him but didn't ask. I decided to ask when it was just Astor, not wanting everyone to stop because of my insecurities.

Beru took a seat in the corner of the room, folding his arms and stared at the ground like a petulant child.

Iri took one look at him, glanced at me, then spoke to everyone. "We all need to get over the issues we have with each other. We must work as a team. To fight for one another without hesitation."

I rolled my eyes, but I knew he was right. We had to work together. Beru had always been there when we'd needed him. I had to give him credit for that. Maybe it was time for me to trust him a little more as well, at least when it came to him having my back.

"I'm ready to fight." Beru stood up and joined the group. He locked eyes with me.

It was uncomfortable, yet I couldn't look away from his fathomless eyes. I nodded silently but felt as if we were exchanging apologies.

"Glad we got that sorted." Astor stood between us, putting his fists on his waist as he smiled proudly. "Now back to the business at hand. She's killed in at least five small villages we know of, but there could be more."

"Has anyone been successful fighting her?" I looked around the room.

Her mouth tightened. "I've only heard of her terrorizing people."

"We don't know enough about her. We need to find out her weaknesses." Iri looked like he would jump out of bed any moment and go off fighting, and I could see from Sade's expression she was worried about him doing just that.

Astor gave my shoulder a gentle squeeze. "And why she wants you."

"I know why she wants me. Dag'draath sent her." I sat down on a free chair to await the barrage of questions I knew were about to hit me.

"How do you know that?" Iri raised an eyebrow.

"She told me."

It was time to come clean to the group. I told them everything, about every dreamwalk and my lack of control in going back to the prison.

Everyone sat in silence until I was done.

"Have you spoken to Runa? This seems like something she should know." Astor bit his lip, visibly worried.

"No, not since our first meeting."

"What does Dag'draath want with you?" Sade's eyes narrowed.

I hoped she still trusted me, but I knew this would challenge that. "I imagine he wants me to help him escape. After all, I freed Beru."

I glanced at him.

He sat in his chair, elbows on his knees, his head hung low, and I couldn't see his face to see what he thought of it. This was at the heart of our disagreement earlier. Would he be angrier now I'd shared with the group, but refused to talk about it with him privately?

A knock on the door startled all of us.

"She's not going to knock on the door, guys." Sade stood up, shaking her head with amusement as she crossed to the door. She opened it, and the healer strode in.

"How is the patient today?" He stopped with a smile when he saw Iri sitting up in bed.

Iri extended his hand for the healer to shake. "I'm fine. Almost back to normal. Thank you for checking on me."

"As I hoped you would be." He turned to me. "Aria, I need to know the components of your ointment. Many villagers have died from these spider attacks. We must save those we can."

"Yes." I took the healer over to the herbs he had left and began mixing up a larger batch. "The key components are all here."

The healer watched as I mixed.

"And these." I took some *trifoliate pratense* from my pocket. "People think they're a nuisance weed, but they work for snake bites and rashes."

"You have experience with it?"

"I remembered the elders in my village using it when a local had been bitten by a snake. Seems it may also work on spider bites." I looked at Iri, who leaned into Sade as she laughed. My cheeks reddened at the sweet moment.

"Yes." The healer smiled as he took what was left of the weeds from my hand. "I'll have one of my helpers scavenge the land for more."

"They shouldn't be hard to find. I know my mom used to make me pick them out of the garden so they wouldn't choke the vegetables." I paused, then gritted my teeth and prepared for the worst. "Can you tell us how bad it is?"

"It's been constant attacks since late yesterday. She's severely decimated the local population."

"I'm sorry this is all happening." I took a deep breath, tempted to give myself to her to make it all stop.

"It isn't your fault. I'm positive we'll defeat her in time."

I could feel my cheeks begin to burn.

He didn't know I was the reason for the attacks. All the deaths were on my shoulders. There was nothing I could do to stop them, except give myself to Widow.

"Umm," I hesitated. "I think I'm the reason Widow is here."

He turned to face me. Placing his large palms on my arms, he rubbed them briskly. "You are not to blame."

"No, I am. Widow wants me." I pushed his hands off, undeserving of the warmth and calmness in them.

He stepped back, eyebrows lowering as he looked at me. "I don't understand."

I couldn't explain everything. Some things had to remain a secret. But I had to tell him why he'd seen so much destruction and why Widow was tearing apart everything he knew.

He returned to packing up his bag with increased urgency.

My heart thudded slowly, painfully as I watched another person lose trust in me. "We're going to make her stop."

"How do you expect to do that?" He was practically shouting and I winced.

I knew I deserved his anger, but it had been nice to feel his pride in me before he'd joined the ranks of those who hated me.

"It's not her fault." Beru moved to stand at my side, his head jutting forward as his hands curled into fists at his sides. He looked ready to tackle the healer to defend me.

Looking at him with the utmost disgust, the healer curled

his lip. "And is it true what they say? You are the traitor Beru she freed from the prison?"

"She was forced to free me." Beru's voice was steady as he regarded the healer. There was something menacing in his sudden stillness.

I practically jumped between them, facing the healer, uncertain if either would take a swing at the other. "I did free him."

He turned and spit on my face.

Beru was on him in an instant, his hands wrapped around his neck, squeezing.

"No, Beru!" I pulled on his arm as hard as I could, practically hanging off him as I tried to break them apart. But he was somewhere else. I wasn't even sure he knew I was there.

Beru backed the healer out of the house and pushed him to the ground, releasing his grip on the man's neck. "You're not welcome here any longer."

Astor grabbed his bag and threw it out the window, avoiding getting in Beru's way at the door.

"You can't do that to him!" They were upset with the wrong person. It wasn't his fault. It was mine. All of this was my fault.

Beru closed the door gently, as if he'd just come inside from a peaceful walk. Bypassing me without acknowledging my horror, he walked back to the bedroom.

I shook with anger at his actions. How dare he treat another healer in such a fashion? One who had just helped to save our friend. I wanted to march in there and put him in his place, but that meant I'd be alone with him. I promised I wouldn't let myself do that again.

"Well, that was interesting." Astor craned his neck to look toward the back bedroom where Beru had disappeared.

"We'll deal with him later. Right now, we need to work as a team and figure out the best way to handle Widow." Iri's reasonable tone brought calmness to the room.

He was right. The drama had to stop. We needed to focus on

Widow and closing the tear in the prison before anyone else escaped.

When another knock came on the door, we all tensed.

Sade moved first and I followed. After the way the healer had reacted, we needed to be ready to protect ourselves from everyone.

The elderly woman who'd rented us the house stood outside, wrapped in a thick wool shawl to protect her from the cool morning.

Sade stepped aside, gesturing for her to enter.

"I come for the dreamwalker." Her voice was reedy and thin, making it sound eerie in the quiet room.

"I'm *a* dreamwalker," I spoke up, not afraid of the frail thing standing at the door. Even if she *were* to suddenly leap at me.

"You must leave. All of you." She looked around the room at us, her face thin and scared. "They are coming for you and will kill us all to get to you."

"We'll be on our way as soon as our friend is well enough to travel." I couldn't argue with her words. She was right.

"No, you must leave today. Now. The sooner, the better. Or everyone around you will pay for your mistakes."

She turned and walked out of the house wordlessly, leaving Sade and me to watch her openmouthed

If we stayed, these people would be murdered.

CHAPTER 15

We traveled for three days, Widow and her spiders never far away. Every town we stopped to rest in reported spider attacks. It seemed at times she knew where we were going before we did.

We were still days from the coast. We slept in shifts after the night we woke to find three bodies suspended over our camp-fire, dead. It was clear she was playing with us.

"He's dead."

Sade and I were washing up at the water's edge when Iri's angry voice called out. I rushed to dress, stumbling up the hill while I put my shoes on. When I got to the top of the hill, I could see one of the horses lying on the ground, stiff and lathered with sweat on his flanks.

"She's heartless," Astor spat, rubbing his face.

"I'm not scared of her." Sade turned to project her voice into the woods. "You won't stop us!"

I brought my hand up, covering my eyes in a futile attempt to soothe the pounding headache from the lack of sleep. "We need to bed down for a couple of days. I can't keep on like this."

Iri swept me up in his big arms and hugged me. "Soon. Once we have gained some ground on her."

I pulled back from him and nodded. I needed to rest now. My body ached from sleeping on the ground, riding a horse all day, and sitting in the carriage. If Widow wasn't chasing us, I would have almost welcomed walking to our destination.

"We'll trade horses in the next town." Beru threw our supplies on the back of the carriage.

"What about him?" I pointed to the dead horse.

Beru shrugged and kept packing.

I knelt and ran my hand through his mane. He didn't deserve this. "I want to bury him."

"There's no time. Besides, he's dead. He won't know the difference." Beru kicked at the fire pit to cover the red-hot coals, then dumped the soapy wash-water on it for good measure.

"Are you that heartless?" I stood and ripped a thick branch off a tree and moved beside the horse. I began to dig so we could roll him into a grave.

Sade grabbed a stick and soon after Astor followed.

Iri was still weak but poured water for us when we needed it. I was so focused on my work I didn't notice when Beru began to help.

It didn't take long working together for us to dig a large enough hole to roll the horse into. We each grabbed a leg, flipped him over, and let gravity do the rest.

"That was energy we couldn't afford." Beru, now covered in sweat, threw his stick to the ground, and returned to breaking down camp without another word.

The rest of us covered the horse and gave a few words of thanks for its help on the journey, then joined him and Iri, and left immediately.

We traded our horses for fresh stock in the next town then promptly left, trying to cover as much ground as we could.

I knew I'd have to attempt dreamwalking soon to borrow

more supplies, but I was trying to put it off because it meant another stop. At least the others could rest while I worked, and I was trying to keep track of everything I borrowed.

If we lived through this, I was determined to repay everyone we took from. Eventually.

"We need more supplies. We only have enough to last until tomorrow." She looked back at me, her brows were knitted together.

I knew what that look meant. I was tired and needed rest, but I couldn't expect them to understand how hard it was on me. After all, it looked like I was sleeping.

We stopped in a secure location off the trail where we found an old shelter with a somewhat comfortable space for me to lie flat.

I was exhausted, so it didn't take long for me to drift off. This time, Astor had found a baron's home. Luckily when I arrived, he was having a dinner party. People were milling about everywhere. I wasn't dressed for the party in my dirty, scuffed clothes, but no one batted an eye when they saw me.

In the banquet hall, a grand feast was laid out on the table. It was clear from the sheer quantity of food the guests at this event had no idea what true hunger felt like. I kept to the outskirts of the room, stuffing what I could into my pack to take back for the others.

I had a pastry in my mouth when two older women, both dressed in miles of silk, walked past.

One of the women scrunched up her nose at my stench.

I hadn't been able to sit in a hot bath for weeks, and apparently that had followed me here.

"They say she's part spider." One of the women said in a conspiratorial tone. "Milk, please." She held her cup out to me.

Apparently, she thought I was the help. I wanted to hear more, so I poured her the milk. She didn't bother to look at me as she grabbed the drink without a thank you.

"I don't believe it. Sounds preposterous to me."

Both women turned their backs to me as they faced the crowd, leaning in to continue whispering to each other. "It's true. My cousin's girlfriend's brother saw it with his own eyes."

The older of the two looked smug.

"They'll never make it here if that's the case," the younger replied.

"Why is that?"

"The baron has plans in case something happens. I'm sure of it. I'd stake my life on it." The younger woman walked off.

"Foolish girl," the older woman said under her breath, shaking her head as she watched the other leave.

"I've seen the spider-woman myself," I hid my dirty hands behind me.

"What was that?" The woman turned around, her nose wrinkling as she looked me over from top to bottom.

"She's real." I wanted to know how much people knew about her.

"You've seen her?" She stepped closer, despite my smell.

"I have, Madame," I wiped off some of the cheese from a puff I'd just stuffed down my throat.

"I told them all she was real, but no one ever listens to me." She sniffed, turning back to scan the crowd.

"Which one is the baron?" I hoped her disdain extended to him.

"The balding fat one in the corner. Look at all those hussies, fawning over him. His wife is standing right there." She held her nose up further in the air. If it was any higher, she'd fall over.

"Do you think he really does have a plan if the spider-woman comes?" I bit into another delightful puff. This one a sweet cream.

She snorted. "Sure, he does. To get his own hide out of here." With that, the old woman retreated into the crowd with her fake smile, instantly gushing over a couple a few feet away as if they were best friends.

I'd heard enough of the town gossip by now. I needed to get the coin and return before I ran out of energy. From the looks of this party, the baron had more coin than he needed. Perhaps I should rob him blind.

I made my way to the hall where I thought his office would be, opening it to find my hunch had been correct. I scoped out the room quickly, then walked over to the bookshelf where Astor had seen the safe.

Behind the statue on the third shelf, I found the hollow book with the red cover, just like he'd said. There was no lock, which surprised me considering the house was full of people. And in the spot where the book had been was a large space, extending far back into the shelf, full of money.

I ditched the food I'd stashed earlier after less than a half seconds debate. I filled the bag and my pockets with coin. The more I saw on my travels of the rampant poverty people were living in, the worse I viewed the rich barons and businessmen whose wealth we were borrowing. If I could have taken it all, I would have.

He didn't deserve any of that coin while people starved.

I lay down on the floor behind the desk, dreamwalking back to the cabin where my friends were waiting just outside.

Sade opened the door. "You're back! How much did you get?"

"Enough to last us for a while." I smiled and dumped the coins out from my pack and pockets.

"Aria. That's incredible amount. How will he not miss this?" She picked up the coin, bringing it up to her nose and inhaling deeply.

"Oh, he'll notice." I offered a mischievous grin and debated over filling her in now or waiting until everyone was there.

"Why did you take so much?"

"We can give what we don't need to the poor. The people who can't afford a cure for Widow's poison."

"Yes, but if we take more, they'll find out and come after us. We don't need more people trying to stop us. We need to focus on the prison."

"I'm still focused on the prison. We'll never see these people again."

I was annoyed she couldn't see the purpose behind my plan. Then again, I didn't think she'd ever been inside one of the houses of the rich.

She'd never experienced the excess they lived in.

Before she could reply, Beru knocked on the door and walked in. "I just wanted to make sure you were back."

I nodded and looked away. He'd disapprove of my plan if she did.

Beru's eyes widened as he saw the coins spread out on the bed. "How many houses did you go to get all that coin?"

"One." Sade rolled her eyes, crossing her arms.

Beru didn't need to say anything. His eyes said it all.

Sade relaxed her arms and turned to the door. "I'm going to round up the others. I feel like fresh meat tonight. Be back soon. Oh, while you're waiting, you can get a fire going."

Before I could protest, she was gone, leaving me alone with him.

He didn't look at me, still captivated by the coins on the bed. "It's dangerous to take this much from one person."

"I know." I laid back on the cot, pushing aside some of the money. I was exhausted and fully intended to sleep while the others went for food.

Beru could tend to the fire for all I cared.

"I heard what you said to Sade before I came in. About giving to the poor."

I looked away, waiting for him to tell me all the reasons it was a terrible idea.

"I think you're on to something. We could get the support of the villagers. They wouldn't be so scared of Widow if we helped them out. Most of them don't know why she's attacking." He sat on a cot on the other side of the room, resting his elbows on his knees.

"You actually agree with me?"

"Yes."

I folded my hands over my stomach, biting my lip as I stared at the water-stained ceiling. "What if we can't fix this? What if there's no way to close the rip?" The words tumbled out, unfiltered, unbidden, but I couldn't hold them back any longer.

"We *will* help the villagers heal their own. We *will* find the key and close off the prison."

His words were matter-of-fact, but when I turned to look at him, he'd shifted so he was lying on his cot looking at the ceiling as well.

"You say it so easily." It was easier to talk to him like this, each on our backs across the room from each other, without any eye contact to make things awkward.

"One step at a time. We'll get there." He stretched then yawned, bringing his hands behind his head. He made rest look easy.

I turned on my side, feeling more comfortable around him. "What if there's no key?"

"Then we make other plans."

How could he be so calm? I couldn't stop thinking about Widow. When I closed my eyes, she was there. I could still smell her foul breath, the brush of her hair on my face.

"You going to be okay?" He interrupted my thoughts, his voice so quiet I could hardly hear him.

"I don't know."

"You're not doing this alone. Remember that."

I dreamwalked alone. But in all the other ways that counted, he was right. They were all willing to follow me into danger without much debate. I couldn't have found a more dedicated group of friends to help me. But my guilt for putting them in harm's way and keeping back details to spare them the truth still plagued me.

He sat up unexpectedly and walked over to my cot, extending his hand for me to take. I hesitated, then looked at him for the first time in days. How I'd missed him. How I wished I knew for certain he was one of the good guys.

"Do you trust me? I mean, really trust me? Go with your instincts." He extended his hand further.

"Yes." I took his hand without hesitation.

He pulled me to my feet and as we stood together, almost touching, it seemed like he would lean in and kiss me. He stared at me, his dark eyes intense, then let go of my hand. "Come with me."

He opened the door and left the cabin as I caught my breath. What would happen if I followed? For a moment, the same loop of fear and uncertainty tried to pull me in, but I just didn't give a damn.

I ran after him.

CHAPTER 16

We raced through the small towns and villages along the way to the coast, dropping coins for the poor and finding healers. We gave them the recipe to cure those bitten by Widow and her spiders, and it felt good to see how happy people were to have our help.

I needed rest, but I couldn't turn down Beru's offer to help me with the poor.

"Thank you." A woman and her children fell to their knees to pick up the coins he threw to the ground.

"Share with the others. We'll bring more when we can." He held on to the horse's reins and nodded to the rest of us. "Time to switch out our horses. These ones need a break."

"We aren't far from the next village."

Sade took the lead, and we veered off the road onto a path that led into the woods. The next village was larger, so we were able to book a few rooms at a local inn. Hopefully, we'd all be able to have a decent rest for a change.

Once I settled in, I laid down in my bed and dreamwalked into the local treasury. Stealing from the rich was becoming second nature. It was easy once I'd seen how they treated those they considered lesser, and once I'd realized they had made their wealth from the sweat of others.

I'd never stolen from a treasury before. It wasn't someone's home, but a secure building where people worked. I hadn't wanted to stick out so, before dreamwalking, I'd looked for a reason why I'd be at the treasury.

At supper, we'd gotten enough information from the inn patrons I'd decided to pretend I was one of the government officials' daughters. When I arrived, I was led inside and brought to the bench to wait for him. As soon as the woman who'd greeted me left, I got up and continued down the hallway to where Astor had seen the vault.

At the end of the hall was a room with four men inside. They were sitting at a table discussing village affairs until they saw me.

One of the men turned to me with a surprised expression. "Can I help you?"

"Yes, I'm waiting for someone, but I needed a washroom." I looked down, hoping they thought I was shy, but really, I was trying to obscure my face.

Another man answered, sarcasm dripping from his voice. "It's down the hall to your left. The door has a large sign that says 'washroom'."

I nodded several times without looking up, closing the door firmly behind me. I wasn't sure how I was going to get in the vault without notice. Weighing my options, I walked down the hall to get a better sense of the layout. I came upon a kitchen with three women eating lunch at a large table.

"You know something's going on between the two of them." One of the women leaned in but didn't bother to whisper.

"I heard his secretary even knows," another woman added, raising her eyebrows.

I turned to leave, but one of the women called out to me. "Are you lost or something, dearie?" She stood up and came toward me.

"I'm just looking for the bathroom. I thought it was this way." I pointed down the hallway.

"Now, wait a minute. I know you from somewhere." The lady walked over to me with narrowed eyes, looking me over from top to toe.

"Umm, I don't think so. I'm not from around here." I tried to leave, but another woman chimed in.

"You look familiar to me, too." She pointed her finger at my face, waving it around in a circle.

"I've never been here. I have one of those faces, I guess." I was getting worried now.

They'd all gotten a good look and I didn't think they'd forget me.

Now what did I do?

"No, I always recognize a face when I've seen one. I've definitely seen you around, but I can't place where." She cocked her head, slowly turning it as she squinted at me.

"I know!" The other lady exclaimed, hopping up and down lightly. "You're the one that's been stealing from the rich and giving to the poor." She laughed, looking proud she'd figured it out.

"I ... I..." I stuttered, unsure how I was going to talk my way out of this one.

"There's a picture of you at the front, and another one down at the bank. You're quite well-known around these parts."

"I see."

I glanced around for an escape route and wondered if I'd be able to get to the bathroom in time to lock it and dreamwalk back to my room at the inn. I hoped the others hadn't been seen around town. If they had a picture of me, there may be pictures of them as well.

"Oh, don't worry. We won't turn you in. Are you here to steal from us too?" She seemed thrilled at the prospect.

"We can help you if you are. We think it's fantastic what you're doing." The lone woman left at the table came to join the others, looking just as eager as the others.

I stared at them as they looked at me with an unexpected willingness to help. Before I even had a chance to gather my thoughts, they began to plan.

"We can use the second vault," the oldest woman said.

"No one is ever down there. And that's the oldest coin, so least likely to be missed," another interjected.

I followed along in amazement as they arranged practically everything for how to hand the coin over to us. Perhaps this would be the easiest heist I had ever done. They led me down to the basement and I waited as they shifted boxes around to find the entrance to the vault they'd decided on.

"Oh, rats. It's locked." One of the women tried to pry it open.

"Let me." I grabbed a metal bar and jabbed it into the door, but it didn't budge. The vault door was cast in iron.

"Somebody must have the key." One of them looked toward the other two.

The oldest of the three pulled out a ring full of keys. "It might be one of these."

"If we do use a key, you must promise to tell people I forced you to open it." I didn't want them to be implicated. Not only would they lose their jobs, but if caught they'd also face losing their places in the community.

"Ohhh! Now that's an exciting tale to tell the grandchildren!" The youngest woman giggled.

The older woman began working systematically, attempting each key on the ring while the rest of us waited. Footsteps sounded above and my stomach rolled at the thought of someone discovering us. After what felt like forever, the door popped open.

"I got it!"

Once the vault was open, all three helped me load up the coins in the sacks I'd brought along. I thanked them and turned to make my way to the bathroom, intending to dreamwalk back to my bedroom at the inn.

"Wait!" One of the women called out after me. "Could you tie us up? It would make for an excellent story."

All three of them were looking at me, excitement at the prospect of being able to say they'd been held up making their eyes sparkle.

I paused, not wanting to spend the time tying them up just for the sake of a story, but they *had* helped me. Not to mention it would serve as protection and verification of their innocence if anyone doubted them. Reluctantly, I complied.

I began to wrap them loosely, but they begged for me to tie them tighter. When I tied them to the center pole, they were nearly giddy with delight. Placing my finger to my lips, I left.

Making my way up the stairs to the bathroom, my sole purpose now was to get to my friends and out of the town before anyone else recognized us.

Beru was the only one awake when I returned. I told him about the posters, and he agreed it was better to gather supplies for our trip now and leave as soon as we were restocked. If they were looking for us, a group would be more conspicuous than two people.

We stopped first at a local livery and bartered for four horses, then gathered enough supplies to last four weeks. Villages wouldn't be as plentiful as we neared our destination. If we were lucky, it would be enough to get us to the coast.

"Thank you. I'll take some of those too." I pointed at a pile of horseshoes. It would be best to take some along in case we needed to re-shoe the horses.

"You be careful out there. Those spiders are getting closer," the man at the counter said.

"It's pretty frightening what's happening. It seems like they're everywhere these days." I wanted to know what he'd heard.

Everywhere we'd gone, people were talking about nothing but the spider attacks. In the last week or so, however, we hadn't arrived anywhere they'd had a firsthand experience with Widow.

We continued to leave coin along with the recipe for the paste with healers anyway.

I hoped she had tired of the game or we'd managed to lose her.

"Yes, we'd never heard of spiders attacking before just recently. By the sounds of it though, it might not be long until they're here." He packed our new supplies into sacks, handing them to Beru with a smile.

The merchant's wife came out of the back room with freshly baked loaves of bread and grabbed another sack. "Please take these as well, as a gift for your kindness to the village."

"Oh, I couldn't." I waved my hands at her. We wanted to give to the poor, not take from them, even if it would be useful.

She pushed the bag closer, so I took it, bowing my head in thanks as we departed.

I was suspicious, based on her actions, the villagers did know who we were. At least it appeared they weren't going to turn us in right away. Not wanting to chance our luck, we filled the carriage with the supplies and returned to the inn.

Once there, we woke everyone, packed our things, and headed out. I looked at the inn regretfully. So much for a good night's sleep for me. Dawn was well underway by the time we reached the edge of town, and people were just beginning to go about their work days.

We each dropped a handful of coins behind us, smiling when shouts of excitement and joy followed us.

As I rode through the forest, I was overwhelmed by the

feeling of being summoned. Against my will, I dreamwalked to the white room where I'd first met with Runa. It didn't matter I tried to resist, because she was powerful enough to pull me into the dream meeting without my permission.

I turned to find her sitting on a golden throne. It was the only piece of furniture in the room, so I stood before her like a peasant.

"Where have you been?" She glared down at me her arms crossed. Her disapproval was clear.

"We have a plan. I've got things under control."

"Well, whatever plan you have, you'd better put it into action quickly. Prisoners have found the break, and several are missing."

Runa stood and walked over to the wall. As she lifted her hands and spread her fingers wide, a vision appeared of several ur'gels leaving through the rip.

"Did they make it through the tunnel?" I knew even though they made it out of the rip, they still had to pass through the tunnel. It was unlikely they could have escaped, given what we had endured to get through the tunnel.

Runa swiped her hands to the left, and the image changed. "Some ur'gels have escaped. We are unsure how many, but there are reports of attacks in the Oubliee Desert. We believe they are gathering people sympathetic to their cause and obtaining modern weapons."

I felt frozen as I watched the images play out across the wall. I hadn't thought the ur'gels would find their way out so soon. I'd hoped we'd have more time.

"There's a key to the prison. The person who held it before has died, and we are on our way to find the new owner."

"Your time is up. These warriors have been in prison for over two hundred years. They've had more than enough opportunity to plan what they'd do if they escaped."

For the first time I wondered if our plan would even work. What if there wasn't a key anymore? Had we wasted our time for nothing?

CHAPTER 17

We pushed through the night to make it to the coast. There was no time to steal from any more barons, governors, or treasuries. Widow would continue her path of destruction unfettered for now.

Beru gazed at the water stretching out in front of us. "We're here."

As difficult as our trip had been, I knew this would be the hardest part of the journey. To get to Bruhier, we still had to pass through the deadly waters of merfolk territory from which many ships never returned. It would be about a day's journey by water if we could find somebody willing to take us.

"Where do we get a boat?" Sade jumped from her horse, looking invigorated now we'd reached our first goal.

"We'll have to find a local to take us. We aren't experienced enough sailors to navigate these waters alone, and even if we were, we'd need a navigator." Beru dismounted his horse and gestured to a path by the water. "Wait here while I try to find someone."

"I've heard about the merfolk, but never expected to cross

paths with one. They're said to be beautiful and enchanting, but not to be trusted." Iri's eyes scanned the water.

"I'm not interested in making new friends. Hopefully, we'll be able to cross without any more encounters." I got down from my horse and found my flask. Taking a large gulp of water, I looked out over the ocean as apprehension filled me.

We spent the next hour lying on the grass as we waited for Beru to return. The wind carried the scent of saltwater toward us and the grass was soft as I lay on it with closed eyes, thankful for the moment of peace.

Astor plucked grass from the ground and made a small pile. "Do you think he'll find someone willing to take us?"

"He won't return until he does." One thing I understood about Beru was if he said he was going to do something he would do it.

Conversation lulled as everyone dozed under the hot early morning sun. But no matter how hard I tried I couldn't sleep. Perhaps it was because I was worried about Beru, or maybe about the odds of Widow finding us.

I rolled onto my side and watched as the others slept peacefully. As much as we needed to get across the water, I was pleased they could rest and rebuild their energy. We had no idea what we'd be facing once we reached Bruhier. I had only blinked for a moment when Beru's voice jolted me awake.

"Get ready!"

"You found a boat?" Astor sat halfway up.

"She'll be coming into the cove soon. We can stable the horses by the docks and find new transportation once we're across."

Beru grabbed the reins of his horse, leading it down the hill past a large tree.

"Will they be safe?" Iri hesitated to take his horse over to the same tree.

"A local family will look after them while we're gone. They'll get paid half now, and the rest when we return and see the horses are still safe."

Beru held out his hand for Iri's reins. He reluctantly passed them over, patting his horse on the flank and nodding in recognition of its service. Sade and Astor followed suit.

"It looks like I made it to the party just in time."

We turned at the unforgettable sound of Widow's voice.

She stood on the embankment alone.

Then we heard the boat arriving on the water. The driver stopped, refusing to dock with the half-spider, half-woman standing near.

"Don't worry. She won't go in the water. She'll be too scared of the merfolk," Beru promised, looking back at the boat in the water.

Some of my fear was replaced by relief. Maybe I could find out why she was chasing us if we had an escape route.

"A boat? Just where do you think you're going, dreamwalker?" Her long legs tapped slowly down the hill toward us, the motion of the seven legs gave me the chills.

"I'm getting away from you." I raised my chin defiantly, hoping I could make it to the water faster than she could make it to me.

She smiled, the cold amusement not reaching her eyes. "That much is clear. But where are you planning to go? You can't get away from me. There's nowhere you can hide I won't find you."

"I'm not telling you that. Besides, the only reason you're following me is you were told to." I had to keep her talking so the others could make it to the boat. I locked eyes with Beru, and he shook his head. I could no longer deny our connect.

"What makes you think I'm not doing exactly what I want? Terrorizing ignorant peasants warms my soul." Widow stopped, her eyes zooming past me to the water. "Ah, what a great day for a sunken boat. Are you sure you've thought this through completely?"

"Very sure." I had to keep her there, away from Sade, Astor, and Iri, so they could make a run toward the boat.

Widow began to spin a web.

My heart rate upped, knowing she'd be able to throw it faster than we could run. I'd have to delay her somehow without becoming caught in her web because it would be nearly impossible to escape. The memory of Iri trapped in it and his desperate brush with death afterward made me grit my teeth.

"I must say, I'm impressed you were able to find more than one person to help you on this mission. From what I hear, not many people want you around these days. Not even your own family. How does that feel, little dreamwalker? Is it painful?" She gave me a look of mock concern, before she burst into wicked laughter.

I held my ground, trying not to let her get to me. I told myself she'd say anything to break me down to achieve whatever her sick plan was. But even so, I had to bite back tears thinking of my family. Had she sent her spiders after them?

Beru stepped in front of me, placing himself between Widow and the rest of us. "You must know that feeling, being surrounded by people who only stay out of fear."

I looked back at the others, giving them a nod.

They sprinted into the water swimming as fast as they could to the boat. Sade and Iri were strong swimmers, but had to turn back for Astor, who was not. They each took an arm and dragged him behind them as they made their way to the boat.

With the others safe, Beru and I spread out so it would be harder for Widow to attack us. He moved to the left as I walked to my right.

Widow smiled when she realized what we were doing and began to clap slowly. "I must congratulate you, Beru. You've managed to break out of prison and finally become valuable. Even if it's for the wrong side."

"I'd never work for your side." He pulled out his sword, spitting on the ground between them.

"Never say never, darling. You don't know how your venture will end." She batted her long eyelashes at him.

Gross. Was she flirting with him? "He's not one of you."

I felt dumb for taking the bait but was unable to stand by and let her speak to him that way. It was an insult to think he'd change sides and fight with her.

"Are you sure of that, little dreamwalker? Do you really know this man?" Her head extended a foot from her body as she tilted it to stare at me.

"He's not a monster." If he had been, I would have discovered it by now. I had to rely on what I knew about him, not what other people said, especially someone as untrustworthy as her.

"Whatever. Let's get back on topic, since you're unwilling to be rational. I need you to do something for me." She retracted her neck, returning to her normal height.

I blinked at her audacity. "We aren't doing anything for you."

She smirked, unbothered by my denial. "I'll take that bet. Now, hear me out."

"I'll listen, but I'm not going to guarantee anything." As much as it pained me, I waited. Maybe she'd tell me what her mission was, though I knew whatever she told me would only be a partial truth, at best. But I was curious to see what kind of hold Dag'draath had over her. Perhaps I could use it to my advantage and somehow gain her trust.

Out of the corner of my eye, I saw Beru's head swing toward me in shock. I kept my eyes on Widow, not wanting her to see our bond. I knew she'd use it against me if she did.

Widow skittered closer, close enough to whisper without Beru hearing her words. "I need to know how to bring down the walls of the prison. If you help me, I can guarantee your place in the new world."

"Why would I want to do that? Do you not know what kind

of people are in there? Do you really think you're going to get a place in the new world if the prison does fall?" I was curious what Dag'draath told her to make her believe she'd have the power to promise me something like that. I was certain he was only using her because she was in the outside world and had fallen for his promises.

"I've seen it. The new world will be different from anything we have now. The leaders will be greater. Life will be glorious and for a limited time, you can choose which side you want to be on." From her expression of adoration as she spoke of the future, it was clear she believed she'd picked the right side.

If I could convince her we were on her side, it might give us enough time to make it to the boat.

She wouldn't be able to follow us, so whatever promises we made wouldn't matter once we were gone.

I hoped Beru would understand. "What would I have to do?"

Widow smiled as she swayed toward me.

I had to steel myself not show fear as she came within arm's reach.

"It's rather simple. You need to dreamwalk to the prison and figure out a way to bring down the walls so everyone can go free." Her hairy arm slid across my shoulders, pulling me into her body.

"I don't know how to bring down the walls. I barely made it out alive with Beru." I allowed myself to lean in, trying to relax my body and show no resistance, though my mind screamed for me to run.

"You'll find a way, I'm certain of it." Her voice murmured sweetly in my ear.

I looked over where Beru had been standing, but he wasn't there any longer. I swung my gaze to the left, then the right. Had he abandoned me?

"Oh, are you looking for Beru? He's right here." Widow

moved slightly away, dangling Beru from a web between two of her back legs. She sniffed disdainfully. "He's rather a snoop."

"Let him down." I tried to keep my voice calm even as I felt the shift in my facial features. I knew if I could look in a mirror it would be the same look Mother gave us when we were fighting.

"We were only talking." She smiled, swinging him back and forth lazily. "He's quite the play thing. I can see why you want to keep him around."

"He's not a toy. If you want me to work with you, he's part of the package." I folded my arms to show my deepening disapproval of her tactics, narrowing my eyes further.

"Fine." The legs she'd been holding him with went limp. He fell head first toward the ground and I gasped. At the last moment, she softened his landing with another one of her legs. "Just kidding. Lighten up already."

I raced over, hesitant to touch her web for fear of getting stuck in it. I looked at her, unsure of what to say to get her to release him, but I didn't have to say anything.

She rolled her eyes and unraveled him.

"Are you all right?" I began to pat him all over to see if she'd injured him in any way.

"I'm fine." He grabbed my head, gently pulled me in for a hug he whispered, "What are you doing?"

"Go along with it," I murmured in his ear, then pulled away.

"Please, I'm going to get sick from this love-fest. Does your wife know about your new lover? Oh, right … she's dead." Widow smiled satisfied, folding her arms, and arching a brow.

Unlike me, Beru didn't react to her words. He looked at her with the same expressionless mask which drove me crazy.

"That's enough." I snapped. "If you want my help, this stops now."

"Fine."

I held out my hand for Beru to take and pulled him up.

"We're going on the boat. I'll figure something out. How can I reach you?"

"No worries. I'll find you." She smiled menacingly, but bowed, gesturing for us to proceed.

We walked as calmly as we could to the water's edge, unsure if she was truly going to let us go, but too afraid to look back in case she saw it as a sign of weakness. As we swam to the boat, I felt her gaze on my back as she watched from the top of the hill.

When I finally stood on the boat and looked back, she waved merrily, as if saying goodbye to old friends.

As the boat moved away from the shore, I heard her voice drift over the waves. "While you're hiding, little dreamwalker, rest assured I'll be here, sharing my gifts with your people."

CHAPTER 18

It was past nightfall by the time we made it to the shores of Bruhier. I'd been on edge the entire time, wondering if merfolk were going to attack us, so the sight of dry land made my heart leap with joy, even if it was half-hidden by clouds. Once on land though, my heart sank as I looked at the landscape.

We were going to have a long climb ahead of us in the dark to get to the plateau.

"Which way do we go? It's impossible to see over the veil." Iri walked back and forth, his eyes trained on the mountain, looking for a way up.

"We go up." Beru began to climb, not bothering to wait to see if we would follow.

The blue moon shone, giving us enough light to follow his lead.

Sade went next, staying an arm's length behind.

Iri held back until they were farther up.

Astor stood behind me as we watched our friends climb. "So, climb until we fall to our death? Great plan."

"Come on. Stay close and you'll be fine." I gave him a little push, then began to climb.

"Why? So you can take me out when you fall? No way. I'll make my own path." He snorted and picked a path to the left of me.

We made our way up to the first plateau and when I reached the edge, Beru leaned over and pulled me up.

Sade and Iri were sitting on some rocks drinking water.

Astor wasn't far behind me.

"Any more ideas?" I poured two glasses of water, passing one to him.

"I'll scout the plateau to see if there are any threats. If not, we'll rest here and go further in the morning. We shouldn't take chances traveling in the dark." Iri stood, and when we agreed, he took Beru with him to scout out the area.

Sade and I gathered wood for a campfire as Astor promptly fell asleep where he sat.

"No one will steal him." She stared down at him, an almost motherly expression crossing her face fleetingly.

I followed her gaze to where he was snoring loudly, curled on his pack and chuckled. "You'd be shattered if they did."

"Maybe, but don't tell him I said that." She sat down, slowly feeding kindling to the fire as she built it higher.

I placed my hand over my heart. "Your secret is safe with me."

"How are you and Beru? You seem to be getting along better."

"Good. I think we have some common ground now. I'm starting to think I trust him."

"That's a big statement."

"Do you trust him?" I tilted my head, watching her face intently. In general, she seemed better at reading people than I was.

Sade was silent, lips pressed together as she took time

answering. "I do. For now. But I'm not sure I can say what he'll do once he feels his debt is repaid."

I didn't have the nerve to agree with her out loud, but it was something I'd worried about as well. There was no way to know how he'd react once he thought he'd given enough of his time. The more I got to know him, the more I wondered if I'd ever feel like it was enough time.

A movement in the bushes distracted us and she looked up, placing a finger to her lips. She threw extra wood on the fire and slid her knife from her pack while I shook Astor awake.

"There's something in the woods. You need to get up, but act like you don't know. Grab your knife before you come over to the fire." I walked back to the fire after Astor nodded his understanding. I caught the branches move again. There was someone definitely watching us.

"Should we surprise them?" I spoke in a low voice as I returned to the fire. "Once Astor joins us?"

"Let's wait until Beru and Iri get back unless they make a move first. We don't know how many there are." Sade shifted slightly for a better view of the bushes but continued to poke the fire as if nothing was happening.

"I wonder how long they've been watching." I turned at the crack of a branch behind me to see Astor stumbling to stand and shook my head. If we were aiming for silent, he was failing miserably.

"What do we do?" Astor squinted at the bushes, not bothering to hide his interest.

"First off, try to be a little more subtle." She pushed him to sit beside her. "Next, we wait for Iri and Beru to return. Can you handle that?"

He put his head down meekly.

We sat around the fire and listened to the noises around us silently after that. There was a gentle breeze blowing, so we had to be extra attentive to the noises around us. I knew the creatures in Bruhier were different and it was possible whoever was watching could be either curious or dangerous.

An arrow shot through the sky and landed in the fire. This was not a peaceful greeting.

We grabbed our weapons, stood shoulder to shoulder, and faced the spot where the arrow originated.

Nothing. The bush had quieted and there was no sign of our invisible attackers. I jumped when another arrow flew past me, hitting the fire from a new angle. We whirled, and I completely expected somebody, or something, to come out of the woods.

"Looks like they want to play with us." Her voice held a hint of irritation as she crept around the fire with narrowed eyes, scouring the trees for the mysterious visitors.

We formed a loose circle, our backs to each other as we tried to keep eyes on as much of the darkness as possible.

When the sound of footfalls on the path reached our ears, Sade lunged. As the intruders broke through the brush, Sade stopped, pulling her knife back as Beru and Iri appeared.

"That's not *quite* the welcome back I was hoping for." Beru held his hands up, an obvious look of surprise plastered on his face.

"There's someone watching us. They shot arrows at the fire, but from different locations. So maybe more than one." She kept her eyes on our surroundings as they drew their swords.

"Only place to go from here is up. Everyone ready on my count?" Iri walked toward the rocky cliff face, leaning nonchalantly against it, prepared to start the climb.

We nodded in agreement. We'd have to leave our things behind. If we tried to gather anything, whoever was watching would know what we were trying to do. We could come back later if we were lucky and didn't go too far up the mountain.

"Run!" Iri ordered, and we made a break for it.

As soon as we hit the cliff face, the attackers came out of the woods.

I turned back to see who we were fighting and my eyes widened. I'd never seen anything like them.

They were more massive than the average ur'gel, and surprisingly faster as well. They shot arrows at us until we were out of reach.

Just when I was beginning to appreciate the reprieve, I looked back to discover they'd slung their bows over their backs and were climbing after us. Same as on the ground, they were faster climbers as well. It wasn't long until they'd caught up. They grabbed at our feet as they tried to pull us down.

A large misshapen ur'gel latched on to my foot and was hanging on it, pulling hard. I lost my handhold but scrabbled and caught a tree root. I used my other leg to swing myself around so I slammed him against the wall.

He lost his grip, and the shriek he let out as he fell to the ground was both satisfying and terrifying, knowing it could have been me instead.

I climbed higher, but the ur'gels just kept coming. Another scaled the side of the mountain beside me, leaping onto my back. I let out a cry of surprise and Beru turned, dropping down to throw it off me.

We were almost to the next cliff, but I couldn't see if there were more at the top and we were climbing into a trap. If we reached the cliff first would we be able to pick them off as they came toward us? As we neared the top, we could see people there.

They didn't resemble the ur'gels at the bottom, and more reassuringly, they appeared to be aiming their arrows at our pursuers and not us.

Sade reached the cliff first and I exhaled in relief as they helped her over.

The guys were next.

As I reached for purchase at the top of the ledge, a hand

pulled me up. I stood, breathing too hard from the exertion to realize our saviors were elves.

Elves who'd encircled us with long, sharp spears and grim expressions.

No one spoke, and we remained still, waiting to find out who their leader was.

The ur'gels kept coming and except for the ones watching us, the elves fought to keep them from making it over the ledge.

When an elf shorter than the others arrived dressed in gold, our guards parted to let him in.

Sword in hand, he raised his chin and looked us over. He stopped and directed his words to Iri. "State your business."

"We have come to look for someone. And right now, to get away from the ur'gels. We greatly appreciate your help with the second goal." Iri placed his weapon on the ground as a sign of peace.

The new elf didn't reply, but instead walked around and gestured with his sword. "I'll ask again. What is your purpose here?"

It appeared he didn't believe Iri.

I stepped in front of the group, hoping he'd listen to me. "We wish no harm. We are merely looking to speak with the High Elves in search of information."

He walked around us again, but became distracted by a handful of ur'gels climbing over the cliff at the same time.

We remained under guard as the rest of the elves fought off the ur'gels using flames and arrows.

In comparison to the smoothly coordinated movements of the elves, the ur'gels appeared disorganized, and seemed easy to defeat.

I watched as several ur'gels separated one of the elves from the rest and attacked in unison. I was about to scream out in warning, but then the elf pulled his belt off. Metal spikes glinted in the light of the moon as he swung it.

When it contacted the first ur'gel, it howled and fell backward off the mountain. The elf swiftly repeated the mesmerizing action with his belt, and the others followed closely behind the first.

With his opponents out of the way, the elf put his belt on and hurried to the aid of two others who were rolling out a cylindrical stone. They pushed it over the side, and screams echoed in symphony with the dull *thud, thud, thud* as it hit several hard objects on the way down.

The ur'gels refused to retreat even as the elves decimated their numbers. There was no mercy and I gathered the elves were forced to protect the cliff on a regular basis from their movements. As I looked at the mountain, I could see built-in bunkers and fortifications facing the cliff. This must be a lookout or guard tower.

Once the ur'gel advance slowed, the gold-suited elf came back to face us. With a wave of his hand, two other elves brought a chair for him to sit on.

"You," he pointed a finger at me, beckoning me closer. "Come here."

I didn't argue, kneeling before his chair, waiting respectfully for him to speak.

"I ask again. What are you doing here? This is not your land. We are not your people."

"We are here looking for a High Elf, or at least, hoping to meet with someone who can answer our questions." I hoped he could see the truth in my eyes. I wasn't here to betray him or his people, but he had to believe me if I hoped to move past these elves.

"Why do you want a High Elf? They do not owe you anything. You have crossed dangerous lands to be here. Your reason must be life-threatening." He leaned in, a look of interest replacing some of the distrust.

"Yes, it is life-threatening for many people, not just my own. It will affect your land as well. We're looking for whoever holds the key."

"I do not know what you mean. What is this key you speak of?" He shook his head, eyebrows knitted together.

"It's a key to the prison. We need your help."

He pursed his lips, then stood and walked away. His chair was removed, but our guards remained, spears raised.

Shoulders slumping, I rejoined the others. It appeared I'd failed to make him understand.

More elves surrounded us with their spears, pushing us closer to the edge of the mountain as they yelled in a language I couldn't understand. As the edge neared, I braced for what was about to happen.

CHAPTER 19

"This way."

After thinking I was about to be pushed over the edge, the path along the side of the cliff was almost anticlimactic.

The elves led us along a winding tunnel that extended from the edge deep into the mountain.

When we arrived on the other side, it was into an open field where they allowed us to walk around freely. We were deep inside of their world now, and it was beautiful. On the other side of the field were buildings far older and taller than I'd ever seen before.

As we approached the village, I could make out carvings in the stone walls, intricate and decorative, as well as those appearing to designate some buildings for different purposes.

Elves walked around in colorful clothing, some with bags and shoes that matched their outfits.

There was an outdoor eatery in the middle of the square, full of elves laughing and having a good time. Large flying ships soared over us in the sky, moving in and out of the clouds above.

Everything about the place in front of me was truly magical, especially the sight of the ships traveling in the sky. I knew I was staring in astonishment as another ship flew over us with three masts, its sails fully open and billowing in the wind. Behind the flying ship was a small flock of dragons. I had to bite my lip to hold back a squeal of delight when I saw three smaller dragons trailing behind.

"Wait here." Beore, one of the elves who'd escorted us from the cliff, brought us to a table at the eatery. "I will see what I can do about your request to meet with a High Elf."

We thanked him and took a seat.

A waitress came over almost instantly and placed food in front of us.

I looked down and my stomach rumbled with hunger before a wave of disappointment washed over me. A bucket of fried eyeballs, bird's feet in what smelled like pickle juice, and another basket I couldn't determine the contents of greeted me. Although I was hungry, I didn't think I'd ever be hungry enough to eat any of the food in front of me.

Iri and Sade dug in, crunching on the bird's feet as I pushed the food further from me in fear I might vomit. "I hope they have better food than this."

"I'm with you on this one," Astor wrinkled his nose in disgust.

We sat in silence as we watched the elves mingling around us. I'd never been around any elves and had only heard bad things about them. Clearly, they weren't all true. It was the most peaceful and beautiful village I'd ever seen.

Sade crunched once more before swallowing, then leaned forward to speak in a low voice. "I hate to be a negative nelly, but we should be thinking of a way to escape if we need to."

"I agree. While I think they'll treat us fairly, we should have a backup plan. The last thing we need is to be thrown into

Widow's loving embrace." Iri continued crunching the bird's feet in a manner that made my stomach flip.

I looked away quickly.

"I don't think they're going to throw us over the side. They've treated us with respect so far." Beru was sitting back in his chair with his arms crossed, avoiding the food as well.

It was the first time we hadn't all agreed on what to do, and since I was the reason we were here, I felt the need to serve as mediator.

"It can't hurt to talk about a backup plan. If we don't need it, great. But if we do, then we have it." I hoped the middle road would placate everyone. I really didn't want to pick sides.

"Do whatever you like." Beru shifted so he appeared to be sitting apart from the rest of us now, even though his chair was the same distance from the table it had been before.

I wondered if he had another alternative reason for being here.

He'd suggested Bruhier in the first place, so maybe he had another plan? But why wouldn't he want an escape route?

"Are you honestly going to sit there and pout like a baby?" Astor demanded, sounding completely unlike his usual joking self.

"It's disloyal given how they've treated us. I don't want any part in thinking they'd betray us." He pushed his chair back and stood.

"We can't leave yet." I automatically stood as well. I wasn't sure why everything was falling apart when we'd worked relatively well until now.

"I'll sit." He took his seat, but remained closed off, his expression not inviting further conversation.

No one spoke, likely afraid to make someone mad.

I thought back to what could have made him upset.

He wasn't acting like his usual self, but I had no clue as to why.

"Did you not like the food?" Beore returned amid the awkward silence and for a moment, we just stared at him.

"Erm, just a little different than what we're used to, that's all," Astor smiled broadly at the helpful elf.

"Oh. Well, I have good news. I spoke to the king, and he's agreed to hear your story in the high court. If you'd care to follow me, I'll take you now." He looked eager to lead us away as he bounced on his toes.

"Thank you. We appreciate your hospitality and assistance." I stood to follow him, earning a shy smile in return.

"It's not every day we get your kind here. I'm excited to hear this grand story as well." He walked swiftly through the town, turning to make sure we were still with him.

I did my best to keep up, practically jogging at times.

As we walked, he gave us a quick tour of the buildings and local elves of importance. He clearly enjoyed living here and took pride in the town.

"Have you ever been outside? Off the mountain, I mean." I was curious. It had been so difficult to get here I couldn't imagine doing this trip again anytime soon.

"Now why would I want to do that? We have everything we need right here. We're safe." He stopped and tilted his head, examining my face for a moment. "You are here because you aren't safe."

"We do need your help." I half-smiled, however I didn't want to impose our problems on him. I wasn't able to deny his presumptions though.

"I'm sure the king will do what he can. But his rule is over our land only, so I don't know if he will be of much help." He stopped in front of a large golden yellow building.

We followed him into the building, taking in the ornate sculptures of long-gone elves and paintings of epic battles in the entryway with silent awe. None of us spoke as we took all the grandeur of the enormous hallway in.

We continued walking through the hall, on elegant Khasa marble flooring and past walls a dark color glinting with the lamplight, unlike any I'd seen before. When we reached two large grey marble stone doors, our guide stopped,

"This is the throne room. You will enter first, but I'll be right behind you. Wait until he speaks to you."

I entered the grand room behind Iri to what appeared to be court in session. There was a supplicant in the center of the room, about ten feet from where a single throne sat.

The king listened with his chin resting on his hand to the young elf in the middle, while rows of elves lined either side.

We were ushered to the side of the room to wait with the others and my spirits sank. Were they all waiting for a turn?

I'd hoped we'd have a chance to speak in private, but I should have known better. Now, I wasn't sure we'd have a chance to ask anything. I turned my attention to the elf currently pleading his case.

It appeared he'd spent many nights courting another elf. Taking her out on expensive dates and showering her with gifts, while she'd only been trying to make an old boyfriend jealous. "She embarrassed me, used me, sullied my name. I ask you have her return everything I gave her and reimburse the cost of the dates. I want the chance to court someone who won't use me for their own advantage. Thank you."

My eyebrows shot up at his request. Would the king really humor his request?

My reaction wasn't uncommon. I could see many of the ladies in the crowd politely muffling their laughter.

The king, on the other hand, showed no reaction to the story at all. When another elf whispered in his ear he sat up straight. "I will deliberate on your case later, Theodosius. You may leave." He waved the young elf away, then gestured for us to approach. "We have a dreamwalker in our midst. You may approach with your party."

We silently followed his command, walking into the center of the aisle toward where the other elf had stood while requesting help from the king.

"I am told you have come a great distance to ask for my help. As such, I will listen to what you have to say." He gestured at me with his staff.

I stepped to the front of the group, moving a few steps closer before giving a low bow. "Thank you for allowing us to speak."

"Tell us the story of the great Widow spider." He tilted his head as the crowd gasped.

I told him everything, holding nothing back. From the very beginning when I had discovered I was a dreamwalker, to breaking into the prison to free Beru, and our journey since to find the Light Woman who we hoped held the key to the prison and would enable us to close the tear before any more damage was done.

When I finished, the king shook his head. "That is quite the story. I'm not certain if I should believe you. It sounds like a story for children to make them behave."

"I assure you it is all true. We are here to humbly request your assistance to find the Light Woman." I looked back at my group.

They were standing proudly as the crowd of elves snickered or outright laughed at our story. It was clear most did not believe what I had said.

I tried again. "We wouldn't risk our lives for a story of make believe. We know there was a High Elf called the Light Woman. She held the key to the prison, but that was a long time ago. We think she passed the key on to another upon her death." I looked around the room to see if my words had been believed but was met by more laughter.

"And who told you about this High Elf who holds such a key?" He banged his staff on the floor to regain control, and the laughter quickly died.

I glanced at Beru.

He'd been the one to tell us the story first, and the old witch had confirmed it. When he felt my gaze, he stepped forward. "It is I who first told them of the Light Woman. I am the one who broke free from the prison where I was held for over two hundred years."

When Beru spoke, the room quieted fully. I wondered how much they knew about the prison and the war which had trapped him there.

The king was silent as he examined Beru from head to toe. He didn't ask questions though, perhaps because he knew about the war and the recent prison break. "You survived two hundred years in that horrible prison?" He motioned for Beru to come closer, looking intrigued in spite of himself.

Beru obeyed, approaching him to speak directly beside his chair.

I waited awkwardly, unable to hear their conversation from where I stood. I hoped whatever they were discussing meant he would help us.

As Beru returned to where the rest of us were waiting, the king shifted and sat up straight in his chair again.

"I have no interest in your wars, and I have no idea where the notion of a Light Woman came from. Rest assured, there has never been this person in the Halls of the High Elves."

When he finished speaking, the elves in the building burst into laughter again, as if they'd merely been waiting for the signal.

"But—" I began, but Beru reached for my arm.

Shaking his head slightly, he pulled me back. "It's no use."

I looked him square in the eye.

His face was blank, and his irritating lack of expression made me wonder if he had sabotaged this visit. Why had he done that? And why had he brought us here in the first place if he'd been planning to do this all along?

CHAPTER 20

B eru and I were invited to have supper with the king in his private quarters.

I was hopeful speaking with him in private would entice him to help us yet, if only I could convince him the Light Woman was real.

"I must admit, I've never heard a story like yours before. I'm surprised a mere woman was able to break into the prison and free such a great warrior." The king held his chalice up in a toast to Beru.

I ignored the slight, biting my tongue for an opportunity to steer the conversation back to finding someone who knew the Light Woman or something about the key.

"Aria is a great warrior. I'm thankful she carried through and was able to free me. Despite my ignorance." Beru smiled at me, his last comment sounding almost like a secret between us.

"I would love to hear this story." He shoved a large drumstick in his mouth, ripping off a piece with gusto.

Beru lowered his head, seeming almost ashamed. "I didn't believe her at first. That I could be freed."

I thought back to my many visits.

He'd ignored me so many times, no matter what I'd said or done. He'd had no faith in my ability to free him, but then again, neither had I at first.

"And now you've freed him? Has the aftermath been worth it?" The king's eyes bored into mine, his drumstick resting on his plate as he waited for me to answer.

"Yes." I agreed quickly, but the truth was I second-guessed myself all the time. Life would have been so much easier had I not broken into the prison. I forced the thought away, knowing I would have done anything to get Gavin back.

"You say yes, but then look away. Your eyes speak a truth different from your words." He looked at Beru, gauging his reaction.

Beru was staring at me, his face pale with an expression I hadn't seen before.

I wondered if I'd said something to hurt him and tried to smooth things over with the truth. "I was thinking about my brother. He's the reason I agreed to dreamwalk in the first place. The ur'gels had taken him as a bargaining chip, after first killing another of my brothers to show me what they were capable of. But it has turned out well, now Gavin is home and we've found an ally in Beru."

"You should not have broken into the prison. It sounds as if you have quite a mess to clean up now. But this is not my war, therefore I cannot help. I wish you luck along your way." He loaded more food onto his plate and shoveled it into his mouth, as though the subject was closed.

I wasn't ready to accept his response. Surely, he must know something.

"You're certain there is no Light Woman?" I glanced between the king and Beru, trying to see if they were hiding something.

"Never to my knowledge." He put his utensils across his plate, ending the subject.

Servants immediately descended to remove everyone's

plates. It was clear, even before Beore, our guide from earlier, entered the room and bowed, it was time for us to leave.

"You won't be safe up here in the clouds if they get free. No one will." I gripped the table as I begged him to believe us.

"We will be safe on the island. Now you may go. I wouldn't want you to climb down the cliffs at night. People have been known to fall." He stood and left the room without a backward glance.

"What are we supposed to do now?"

I turned to Beru, frustrated and scared. I hated having to tell the others we'd failed. There was no backup plan to finding the Light Woman, and I didn't have any idea what to try next. I swallowed, wondering if working with Runa would end up being my only option.

"It was a long time ago. We need to keep asking people," he leaned over to whisper so Beore wouldn't hear.

"I'll take you to the veil. You're on your own from there, but we can do a little exploring before you leave if you'd like." Beore's wide, friendly face made me smile. Clearly, our elf guide was eager to show off his home some more.

"Thank you, we'd appreciate that." Beru placed his hand on the small of my back, gently pushing me forward. The contact caught me off guard and I almost stumbled.

"You know, you could take a ship. The king only said you had to leave, he never said how." Beore practically skipped as we walked through town.

"How would we go about getting a ship? I saw them earlier and I didn't even know they existed until then. We don't have anything like them on the mainland." I tried my best to keep up with him while Beru stayed a few feet back, looking around with an alertness more suited to a battlefield than exploring a new place.

"Oh! They are simply the best way to travel. I couldn't imagine not seeing them in the sky every day. Most of them are luxury boats with captains for hire. I'm sure I could get you passage aboard one, if you're interested." He stopped, visibly vibrating with excitement at the idea.

"That sounds exactly like what we need. We could avoid any contact with ur'gels on the way down." I looked to see if Beru agreed, but he was looking at the ground and seemed uninterested in my conversation.

"You wouldn't be able to steal one though." When I gave Beore a sharp look, he smiled sheepishly. "Sorry, I was listening in on your story earlier. Your adventure sounded extremely dangerous, although I think what you did was wonderful. You must be highly popular with the poor in your land."

"I'm not sure I'd use the word popular, but people seemed to appreciate the help we were able to provide." I smiled at the guide's interpretation of our story. "Don't worry. We wouldn't steal one. If you can find us a flying boat to the mainland though, it would help immensely."

"I will do my best. I heard you mention you're a dreamwalker. We have protections against all forms of magic here, which includes the abilities of dreamwalkers. If you attempt to use your abilities here, they simply will not work. It's one of the many protections we have to help lower the risk of attack by outsiders." Beore continued along the path through town, chatting as he occasionally pointed out interesting places.

That explained why I'd been unable to check in on my parents. I couldn't even enter the dream realm, which I'd only thought was because I was overtired. But realizing I was blocked made me wonder about other things. Did they have healers? Could any of the residents do magic? I had a difficult time imagining what a land without magic would be like.

"Could you take us to our friends? We'll pack our belongings while you find us a ship."

"Certainly! Follow that path to the large stone house beside the water wheel. Your friends have been given food and lodging there."

We left him, following his limited directions easily. Neither of us attempted small talk, and I couldn't help but wonder why he had been acting so differently since our arrival. Had something happened? Finally, I couldn't hold my questions back any longer.

"Were you surprised by the king's decision?"

"I thought he would have known about the Light Woman, but it has been a long time." He kept his hands in his pockets and walked at a slow, relaxed pace without looking at me.

"You seem pretty nonchalant, considering this was your idea."

"What does that mean? Should I be acting more emotional, like you?" He stopped in the middle of the street, narrowing his eyes at me, waiting for a response.

"Emotional like me? We've traveled weeks to get here to see this Light Woman, which you told us about, but no one has ever heard of her." I flung my hands in the air, frustrated.

"I knew her two hundred years ago, and she was ancient then. I can't help if she no longer walks upon Lynia." Beru turned away and began to walk faster.

It looked like he had finished answering my questions the way he stayed at least three paces ahead even as I jogged to catch up. We arrived at the stone house just as our party waw leaving.

"That was a long supper," Sade adjusted her pack, raising an eyebrow. "We received a message we're leaving by airship and to meet our elf guide at the wharf."

"We packed your stuff. We weren't sure if you were going to meet us there or come back." Iri smiled, handing me my bag.

"Thanks," I muttered, surprised they'd heard the plan before we'd gotten a chance to tell them. We'd only just left Beore.

Suddenly suspicious the airship had been prearranged, I glared at Beru.

He ignored me, focusing instead on the hand-drawn map Iri was showing him of the town and plateau area.

"The docks are on the other end of town from here. Let's go." They led us away from the house, into the city.

As we walked, I was still amazed by how tall the buildings were, up to five and six stories. The sidewalks were made from some sort of hard material they had painted bright red, and color was everywhere.

As we walked, we passed elves and humans, all going about their business. The elves we passed were speaking what I assumed was Elvish, but overall it seemed to be a place of harmony.

I was impressed, as elsewhere in Lynia humans and elves often had strained relations with each other, let alone other creatures. But here, all signs pointed to an integrated, welcoming society.

Maybe things weren't so bad without magic.

We paused at a waterfall and I soaked in the relaxed atmosphere it provided in the small square. The gentle humming was soothing to my frayed emotions. When it met up with the gentle bubbling of a small river, I laughed out loud as a fish jumped out and nearly hit me as we crossed over one of the many small bridges.

"This way." Sade pulled on my arm to direct me.

I was so busy looking at the architecture, I hadn't been paying attention to where we were going, and I realized we were at the end of the street and Iri was almost out of sight.

"Right!" I jumped over a stone marking the end of a street and jogged to keep up with his long legs.

"It should be just over this hill." She broke into a run as she reached the top, then began to jump up and down. "You're not going to believe this!"

I ran to join her, my own excitement swelling. It wasn't every day she looked excited about anything. As I rounded the top of the hill, I thought I was in a dream.

The docks weren't like anything I had ever seen before. There was no water for the boats to float on, instead clouds shimmered where the water should be, and airships filled the docks as far as I could see. Ladders, ropes, and nets flowed off the sides of them to the docks below. Instead of anchors they moored them to the docks via an assortment of ropes to a central attachment near the boardwalk on the island. It was breathtaking.

Astor grabbed my arm tightly. "I'm scared of heights."

I laughed at his expression before shaking his arm off to run down the hill after her. Wet red dust covered my feet and legs as we pounded down the roadway and I felt more alive and freer than I had in a long time.

"It's boat eighty-nine," she was almost gasping by the time we reached the boardwalk, and we searched what seemed like a hundred ships for the number.

Her eyes sharpened, and she ran over to a post at the end of the dock where I saw Beore waiting for us. "Over here!"

"Is this us?"

"No. Your vessel is one of the largest here. The edge is silver, the body is green. Trust me, you can't miss it." The elf shaded his eyes from the sun with a hand as he leaned over to peer through the port. "I don't see it yet."

"Does it always park in the same place?" Sade walked over to look in another lane.

"Wherever she can fit, generally."

"They know we're waiting for them?"

"Yes, commission already purchased, compliments of the king." His eyes twinkled, leaving me with the feeling there was something he wasn't telling us. "I've got to get back to court now, but I wish you the best of luck on your journey." He bowed, then darted off again.

"This place is amazing. The boat can be as late as it wants." Sade's eyes were big as she turned from side to side, trying to drink it all in.

I glanced at Beru.

He stood off to the side, seemingly uninterested in any of the amazing sights around us.

I couldn't help but wonder if maybe it was because none of this was new to him.

"Let's walk around. I'd like to get a better look at some of these boats."

Iri didn't bother to wait for a reply. He headed over to the fancier, multilevel flying ships, some of which appeared to be lived on. The guys followed him, but Sade and I hung back to wait.

I was content to enjoy the view, and Sade didn't want to miss our ship.

"This is pretty freakin' incredible!" She sat on the edge of a bench on the boardwalk, shaking her head in wonder. "I still can't believe we get to go up in one of these."

"Yeah." But as beautiful and awe-inspiring as the docks were, I couldn't stop thinking about Beru. I should have been studying the details of Bruhier to tell my grandchildren one day, but here I was, fixated on his past.

CHAPTER 21

"Don't look now, but I think that woman is staring at us."

I followed her gaze to a human who stood across the boardwalk, doing exactly what she'd just told me not to and earning a smack on the arm. I winced. "Maybe we remind her of someone?"

"Or maybe she's a crazy stalker killer lady." Sade inched closer, her gaze darting between the woman and where the guys had meandered off to.

"You're scared of a human, but you'll fight and kill monsters without flinching." I pulled back to see her expression better, amused at the unexpected new quirk she'd revealed.

"She's not moving. At all. She's literally just standing there, staring." Sade clutched at her hands as she leaned in closer on the bench and I laughed.

"Why don't we put your imagination to rest and go talk to her?" I stood, letting out an impatient huff when she shrank back. "Oh, come on. I'm sure she won't kill us in broad daylight."

"Fine." She stood but pushed me ahead a few feet. "You're going first."

I rolled my eyes, turning to walk confidently toward the woman.

She didn't move even after it became clear we were approaching her.

"Hello!" I called when we were closer.

She didn't respond, however her eyes remained firmly fixed on us.

Sade pulled on the back of my shirt, her steps faltering. "Are you sure we should do this?"

I looked back curiously, confused by how genuinely scared she seemed of a mere human, and one who was smaller than either of us at that. "Are you serious right now?"

Sade folded her arms, setting her mouth in a firm line. "It's your death."

I wrinkled my forehead, wondering what had gotten into her. Now even more curious, I turned and extended my hand as Sade kept her distance.

"I'm Aria. I noticed you seemed to be watching us. Is there something we can help you with?" I stepped closer, and she stepped back.

"We can't talk here." The woman looked around, fiddling with her necklace as she checked for eavesdroppers. "Follow me. We should speak somewhere more private."

I looked back at Sade. She was several feet back now, her arms firmly crossed as she watched with wide eyes.

"Before I do that, I need some information. Like your name to start with." I wasn't clueless enough to go anywhere with this woman, even if I thought Sade was overreacting.

"I'm the captain of the ship hired for you. You may call me Captain Rose." She finally extended her hand, but still seemed skittish.

"We were just looking for your ship. Our guide thought you hadn't landed yet." I exhaled in relief, feeling completely foolish for letting Sade get in my head.

Abruptly, she leaned over to hug me. Caught off guard, I instinctively tried to push her away, but she held on with a surprisingly strong grip for someone so delicate.

"I know where you need to go." She whispered in my ear. "I know about the Light Woman, but we can't speak of it in the open. Too many ears." She pulled away, almost wild-eyed, smelling of dirt and roses.

I sneezed as the scent aggravated my nostrils and before I could react, she took off into the crowd. Sade joined me, linking her arm in mine as she whispered in my ear.

"Why did she hug you? Who is she?"

"She says knows the Light Woman but doesn't think it's safe to talk in the open. She's also the captain of our ship, apparently."

I kept my eyes on the woman as she wove her way through the crowd, trying not to lose sight of her. She moved fast, considering the boardwalk was full of people milling about.

"So, we have to go up into the sky with her?" Sade halted abruptly, eyes wide.

I coaxed her to continue, practically dragging her for a few steps. "Yes. But we aren't going back to the mainland. She said she knows where to go to find her."

"Yeah, to the gods in the sky, where she'll sacrifice us." Sade huffed, grudgingly resuming her previous pace even as she sighed dramatically.

"Look, this is exactly why we came to Bruhier in the first place. I'm sure everything is going to be fine. She's not that scary." I turned to look for Captain Rose and found her standing under the most beautiful vessel I'd ever seen. Beore had told us it was big, but I hadn't been prepared for how massive it actually was.

As we neared the ship, I could make out scrollwork on the bottom. It was intricately carved with scenes depicting people and places in a way that made me want to read it.

The carvings were interconnected, and I knew they told a story.

I was distracted from my attempt to read it by the presence of three giants loading the boat with supplies. With three jumps up the rope ladder, they could make it to the top with ease while carrying supplies in both hands, singing as they worked.

"Looks like you beat us!" Iri waved from across the boardwalk as the guys walked toward us from the opposite direction.

"I'm not going up there." Astor's face was pale, his entire body trembling as he watched the giants on the rope ladder.

"Just don't look down." Iri slapped him on the shoulder, a broad smile on his face. "I'll even go behind you, in case I need to catch you."

"Either die falling or get murdered on board. I'd rather take the fall. At least it's a nice view." Sade shivered.

I gave her a pointed look which she ignored, then turned to the others. "Let's go. I'm eager to head out." I called out to Captain Rose, who was still supervising the giants. "Can we board yet?"

She held out her hand. "You must pay the fee first."

I reached into my pack my eyes narrowed. "I thought the fare was already paid by the king?"

She shook her head absently as she looked at my bag. "What do you have in there?" She peered into my pack. "That'll do." She grabbed the entire bag of coins out of my hand.

"Hey, wait a minute. That's all that we have." I reached for her, but she pulled away.

Leaning over so she could speak low enough only for my ears, she gave me a warning look. "Do you want me to take you to the Light Woman or not? He may have paid for the ship, but not my time. If I take you to her, I'm risking my privilege to land in Bruhier, and it needs to be worth it."

I searched her eyes, relaxing my shoulders as I nodded. After all, it was only money. I stepped back, allowing her to take it without arguing further.

She smirked, then pointed to the rope. "Hoist yourselves up the best you can."

She flung my pack up to a giant who caught it in his hand, then lobbed it up and over the side before following close behind.

"That was all we had." Sade's voice was full of dismay.

"We can get more later. Let's go before her fee gets any bigger."

I went first. The giants made it look easy, but the moment I began the climb I knew it was their weight doing it. The ropes were flimsy and moved with the wind, and with my lesser mass it swayed uncomfortably. I regretted filling my belly at supper as it lurched into my throat.

As I climbed higher into the clouds themselves, I looked down. I couldn't see anything past my feet. Stopping to enjoy the cool mist making my skin tingle, it seemed to me I was floating in a puff of cold cloud.

I closed my eyes to enjoy the sensation of clean freshness, noticing a whooshing noise which seemed to be getting closer. I opened my eyes and looked around but saw nothing. Suddenly it began to get warmer, and I felt a large gust of hot air pass, before the broad wings of a dragon entered my field of vision. I clung to the rope as it flew by, causing the ladder to sway alarmingly from side to side.

It was the motivation I needed to move faster. I climbed the rest of the way as quickly as I could, ready to stand on something firm. When I was almost at the ship, a giant leaned over to grab my hand, pulling me aboard with my entire arm between his thumb and forefinger coincidentally.

"Thank you." I watched as he pulled my friends over the railing one by one, Astor last.

His eyes covered, I realized Iri must have had to climb the

entire way hobbled by Astor clinging to him by the way he was acting.

"I'm never leaving this boat," he moaned loudly, wobbling over to a bench and collapsing onto his back. He closed his eyes and draped his arm over his face.

I looked at Iri with a raised eyebrow, but he was stoically brushing himself off, and seemed unbothered by Astor's rendition of a dramatically dying goat.

Captain Rose was the last to board. She swung herself over and headed to the helm without looking at us.

"That's probably where she kills people," Sade whimpered.

"Seriously? Can we get over the murder stories already?"

I walked to the edge of the ship to peer over the side as the giants pulled up the rope ladder. There was no turning back now, even if we wanted. We were at the mercy of Captain Rose.

THE ROAR of the engine drowned out both Astor's moans and Sade's whimpers. A large puff of grey smoke plumed out of a metal tube, and after a clunk, it smoothly pulled out of the harbor.

As we flew away from the mountain, the sky cleared of clouds and the vista opened wide below us. It was clear for miles, and for the first time I was able to clearly glimpse Bruhier. It was stunning. Above the veil it was possible to see the island was composed of a multitude of plateaus, not just the one we'd been on.

We cruised along through the traffic, moving slowly but steadily. I watched dragon riders and saw what I thought were Avians for the first time. If I was right, they were a product of High Dragons and other races coupling. They were stunning creatures. I'd heard they had an affinity for magic and could bond with dragons. Being able to see them in their element was incredible.

Beru tapped my shoulder. "Captain Rose wants to speak with you in her cabin."

His tap was the most intimate he'd been since we'd arrived in Bruhier.

It startled me enough I could only nod. I headed to her cabin, but as I was about to knock, the door swung open.

"Close it behind you." She was standing with her back to the door, looking over maps on a large, slanted table.

I looked around the room, amazed at the items contained on the shelves and in cabinets. Everything was either bolted down or latched shut, which I imagined was necessary in case of turbulence.

Every inch of the walls were covered in paintings, drawings, or maps. One wall was covered in shelves filled with more books than I had ever seen in one place. The bed beneath the window was a simple wooden pallet piled high with blankets and pillows, with drawers for storage below.

"Have a seat." She pointed to a small table in the corner with two seats.

"You've got an amazing collection." I sat down as she pulled out two glasses from a small cupboard beneath the table then grabbed a small bottle of amber liquid from a shelf above her head.

"Would you like a drink?" She filled both glasses before I could answer.

"Sure," I lied. I'd never been one for alcohol, but I knew it was sometimes safer than water, from a healer's perspective at least.

"I'll get right to it. Everyone's been gossiping about the dreamwalker who came to Bruhier searching for the Light Woman." She plopped down in her chair, then grabbed a bowl of nuts, and threw it on the table in my general direction. "Food."

"Thanks." I looked down at the bowl, wrinkling my nose at the dust. "Been a while since you had company?"

"You could say that."

"I'll assuming you heard about the prison break swirling through the gossip, too?" I pushed the bowl away, electing to take a sip from my cup instead. The liquid burned as it traveled down my throat to my stomach. Whiskey. Well-aged, too.

"Yup, heard that, too." She slammed back her cup in one gulp. "I've got my own thoughts on that."

"You don't agree?"

"I'm more interested in what you want with the Light Woman."

"So, there is a Light Woman?" Relief Beru hadn't lied flowed through me at her words.

"Yes, there's a long line of Light Women."

I examined her face carefully.

She had wrinkles at the corners of silver flecked green eyes, her sun and wind-beaten face showed laugh lines. She couldn't have been more than thirty, so I was sure it couldn't be her.

"We were told she'd passed away. Is that true?"

"Depends on which one you're talking about." She sat back in her chair, crossing one leg over the other's knee.

I couldn't read her expression. Was it hard for her to talk about this? "I'm sorry, are you saying there's more than one?"

"What do you need her for?"

"She holds an important key to the prison. I'm hoping she can help us close it."

She did a double-take, both feet slapping the floor hard. "Did you leave it open?"

"Not intentionally. We weren't aware of it at the time, but somehow it ripped. Prisoners have started to escape, and more will follow once they find out."

She stood abruptly, her chair rocking back, almost tipping

over as she went to the shelf with the whiskey bottle. Instead of filling her cup, she drank straight from the bottle.

I couldn't speak, alarmed at her reaction and wondering if I should leave. I looked toward the door but decided against it. Even if I left her cabin, it was impossible to leave the ship.

We were at her mercy, whatever her plan was.

"I am a descendant of the original Light Woman. It was important to have the key passed on to someone who understood what it was. You see, it's a well-known fact in my family, one day someone would be stupid enough to open the prison and let Dag'draath out."

CHAPTER 22

While Captain Rose shared her opinion of what I had done, openly and at length, she also offered to bring us to someone willing to help. She was the first person we'd met who understood the degree of difficulty we'd be in if we couldn't repair the rip in the prison, so I bit my tongue at her less than flattering sentiments.

"It's just off these mountains," she called from the wheel of the ship, pointing to the right as a small island came into view below the clouds.

"Who are you taking us to see?" I laid my head on my hands on the side of the ship. I looked at the view from the ship, stunned by the beauty around us.

"My sister. She's the only one who can help." She made a hard turn, and everyone held on as chairs and tables toppled over on the deck. "That's for your friend." She winked, pointing at Astor, who'd turned a deeper shade of green.

"Does your sister have the key?" I was eager to find out more.

"I'll let her tell you. We're almost there." She turned to shout out at the crew. "Haul off!"

The giants pulled hard on the ship's ropes and I felt the ship lurch as it began to slow.

She turned the wheel again, and now we were positioned precisely over the small wharf in front of us.

One of the giants hauled out the long rope ladder and threw it over the side.

"Will you wait for us?" I turned back to her before I went over the side, hoping she didn't expect more money.

She'd nearly cleaned us out already. "My sister would kill me if I left you here." She smiled though, looking tempted by the thought.

I lifted my leg over the edge of the boat and fished around for the ladder, somewhat reassured we wouldn't get stranded. I climbed down, finding it easier than going up. I watched as my friends descended, while Iri brought up the tail, again carrying Astor, but this time on his back like a child.

I shook my head at how he was acting, but all thoughts of his behavior fled when I turned to see a woman with long, flowing white hair dressed in a long pink robe waiting for us at the end of the pier.

"Welcome to the Island of the Temple." She held out her hands, cupping them together as a light appeared in her palms.

"These are the idiots who broke the prison. They're here to talk to Lunla." Captain Rose jumped off the rope ladder and landed lightly on the ground behind us.

"Your sister is waiting to talk to the dreamwalker." The woman extended her arm in the direction of the temple. "Your friends may wait here for your return."

I looked at them and Sade nodded. For some reason, I wasn't afraid to go with this woman. I assumed she must be a priest.

Her energy was so calm and peaceful I instantly felt at home. The magic ban the High Elves had in place must not reach this far.

I followed her along the sandy path. She was barefoot, and

her gown flowed like the petals of a rose as her skin caught the light. She looked like a goddess, like she belonged to the land.

"Do you all live on this island?" I had so many questions I didn't know where to begin.

She turned, smiling as she gestured to the building we'd just departed. "Yes, we stay within the temple grounds. The island suits our needs perfectly."

As we approached the second temple, colorful flowers framed the small garden, many of which were unfamiliar to me. I was distracted from their beauty by men and women playing a game in the grass, tossing a small wooden ball through round hoops.

"Do you play gronnet?" The priestess turned back to me.

"I've never heard of it. Is that what they're doing?" I pointed toward the players as I stopped to watch.

"Yes, it's one of our traditional games. It's very strategic." She folded her hands in front of her, her face serene as she waited for me to watch my fill.

"I'd like to learn." I smiled inwardly, excited at the prospect of learning a new game.

"I would be happy to facilitate that, once you've met with Lunla."

I looked at the group, noticing a young man had stopped playing, watching me with a closed, unfriendly expression. I walked a little faster, reminding myself not for the first time since coming to Bruhier, these weren't my people, and many were upset with me.

We came across some young girls and boys playing tag. They looked like any other group of children playing, giggling, and teasing each other, except for their ability to fly and climb trees like a lion. They all wore the same long red cloak with white underdresses, no matter their gender.

"Do you have any healers here? I noticed an abundance of

herbs and plants any healer would be proud to have in their garden."

"We are taught to heal as children. We don't have many chances to practice as we rarely get sick. Perhaps it is because we do not leave the island and rarely have visitors. Today is a special treat." She smiled, continuing to glide along with a slow and steady pace. It was clear from how everyone was acting there was no rush on this island.

Directly in front of the second temple was a garden even more expansive then the first, protected by a glowing, translucent, white wall. The plants lined the ground in neat rows, and it was tempting to touch the glowing wall, but I didn't want to get in trouble. I was curious as to what magic kept it up, and what exactly were they trying to keep safe.

The priest noticed my expression and as if she could read my mind, pointed to the garden. "Our sacred medical garden. The children are taught to heal almost any sickness from the trees, herbs, and flowers within the walls." She nudged me along the sandy path. "Come, we are almost there."

"How is it you're able to use magic here? I haven't been able to use mine since coming to Bruhier. The High Elves said they blocked all use of it without permission."

"They have no jurisdiction here, although they have tried. This is our land, and we do allow some magic here. It is still controlled and monitored though, and if anyone uses it against our treaty with the High Elves they will be stopped." She looked at me sternly.

I read the warning in her eyes and rushed to reassure her of my intentions. "I'd never use my abilities to hurt any of you. I just want to fix what has been broken and appreciate whatever assistance you can offer."

"We're here." She stopped in front of the temple. "You may go inside. I shall wait here to take you back to the ship when you have finished."

"Thank you for bringing me here," I bowed low before entering the building through two large elliptical doors. As I approached, they swung open to reveal a sun-dappled room. I looked around cautiously, expecting to see someone there, but other than ornate wooden sculptures in the corners, I was alone.

Instantly the scent of wildflowers filled the room and candles blazed to life in candelabras.

I realized I was so enthralled with the golden beauty of the room I hadn't noticed a small woman standing off to the side.

"You must be Aria. I am Lunla." Her skin was pale, and she had striking raven-black hair with alabaster skin. Dressed in a long white gown, the only physical attribute she shared with Captain Rose was the color of her eyes.

"You're Captain Rose's sister?" I was relieved when she accepted my nervously extended hand. What was the proper etiquette for meeting a high priestess?

"Yes, Rose is my sister. I hope your trip here was peaceful. I am eager to discuss things with you." She offered me a chair, sitting in the one beside it in front of a tranquil waterfall.

"This is incredible. I can almost feel the energy from the water soothing and restoring me." Water was the perfect energy conductor. It was an ever-flowing source of traction to harness and drain energy sources.

"It was a must for the creation of this temple. This waterfall has flowed for many centuries and contains the energies of our ancestors." She held her hands up to the water and the water curved slightly as if she drew to her body.

"Your ancestors are the Light Women?"

"Yes, and they were much more. I've been following your story. We knew the day would come and want to thank you for freeing Beru. Few understand how important it is for him to be out of the prison."

She turned toward me and I felt at peace with myself and my

decision. It was so overwhelming tears sprang to my eyes. Finally, somebody understood what I'd had to do. She leaned over and wiped my tears with her hand.

In doing so, she shared some of her energy with me. I closed my eyes, letting it tangle with mine. The restlessness I'd felt these past few weeks healed itself. I no longer felt tired and exhausted. Her energy revived and reinforced my drive to repair the rip.

Lunla removed her hand and smiled with half-lidded eyes. "Now, you must tell me everything you know about the prison."

I took a big gulp and tried to figure out where to begin. "When I freed Beru, I didn't realize we'd left a tear in the prison. Some of the other prisoners have found this and escaped. We need the key to lock the prison again."

"Why do you think the key will fix the rip?"

"Because it keeps the prison closed. There has to be a way that it can help fix it."

"I'm sorry if that is the reason you've come. As much as it is powerful, the key cannot fix the rip. It has an entirely different purpose."

She must be mistaken. We'd spent all this time trying to find her and the key. She had to be able to fix it. She must know a way to fix it.

"I don't understand."

"I don't think you know what the Light Woman represents and what she's capable of."

At her calm response, my heart began to pound. "But there has to be something. We can't let them all out." We had to find a way to fix the tear, whether it was with the key or not.

"The walls of the prison were created from a sacrifice of a powerful mage warrior with the help of most of the high dragons. There's no way to recreate that."

She stood and walked to a wall with hundreds of candles. She picked up one of the lit candles and lit three more. "These candles burn in memory of our ancestors. We must seek the truth through them."

"Can you find out how to fix the prison?" I barely stopped myself from begging on my knees. She was trying to guide me, but I was still reeling from disappointment.

"You must let the walls fall, slowly." She lit four more candles. "Then you must stop Dag'draath."

"But how can I do that? If the walls come down, there's no way to control anyone leaving."

"The answer is Beru. You must fix him."

CHAPTER 23

"To heal Beru's soul, you need to dreamwalk. He is the key, but he is not yet up to the challenge. Unless he can be healed, he will be incapable of doing what needs to be done."

I sat in silence as I processed what she said. After a moment, I shook my head. "I still don't understand. Wouldn't he know if he was the key?" Maybe that was why he'd been acting so strange lately. Did he remember something from his past?

"He does not know. He lost his way during the centuries in the prison and we must guide him back to his task. We must help him tap into the energy he needs to be the person he was born to be."

She obviously didn't know him. "And you're positive he's the key? No chance it could be anyone else?"

"You've grown close." She came back from the wall and sat across from me, watching my face with a calm, sympathetic look as if she could see all my inner turmoil.

"I wouldn't say close exactly, but I feel like I know him. I've had a connection to him, ever since the first time I saw him."

But did I really know him? How close was our connection if I wasn't even sure how he would take the news *he* was the key?

"Relationships can surprise us." Lunla smoothed out the wrinkles sitting had created in her robe, her expression one of deep thought. "At times, you may discover something you weren't looking for."

"I guess." I did find something in Beru. There were fleeting moments where it seemed we were inseparable, even if lately it seemed we were always at odds.

"May I suggest you keep this news to yourself? Just for now, until he's ready." She cocked an eyebrow as she stood, then gestured for me to follow her.

I guessed our time was over. I kicked myself for wasting time and not asking more questions, but I'd been too shocked about finding out Beru was the key. "How will I reach you again? I'm not sure when he will be ready, and we don't have much time. Prisoners are already escaping."

She embraced me. Roses and sunshine filled my senses as she pulled back. "Rose will be our connection. You are a healer and will find a way to reach Beru. You *must* trust your abilities."

I turned toward the exit, bowing my thanks, but feeling uneasy and even more unprepared than I had before meeting her. How was I supposed to fix him? What did she mean, exactly?

We hadn't been getting along, so the chances of him allowing me to help him remember with a healing seemed far-fetched.

I stood in the sun for a moment, appreciating its warmth. I wished it could burn away my confusion but the sound of Sade laughing in the distance brought me back. Maybe she could help me convince him to do a healing.

I walked toward where she stood with Captain Rose. "Sade!"

She didn't hear me, engrossed in whatever conversation they were having. Even when I was right beside her and tugged on her shirt, she didn't take my hint.

"That's amazing!" Sade squealed as Rose pulled out a small carved figure from her jacket.

Sade laughed as she told a story of a one-legged man and I nodded and smiled, trying to get her attention, but nothing worked. She was very interested in Rose, and not so much in what I had to say.

I pressed my lips together, narrowing my eyes as I looked around.

Beru and Astor sat across the garden having tea with a beautiful priestess. They seemed as enraptured with her as Sade was with Rose.

I looked away, not wanting him to think I was jealous if he caught me staring. That left only Iri to talk to. I couldn't see him in the small garden with the others, so decided to find him while I took a walk to clear my head. I needed to figure out what to do about this new development. While I'd wanted to talk it over with Sade, maybe I'd have more luck convincing the others if I had the makings of a plan first.

Taking the path through the woods, I used my senses to follow Iri's energy. I realized I was enjoying the time alone and couldn't remember the last time I'd had a moment to myself. Feeling the need to be closer to the earth, I removed my dirty, crusted boots and socks and continued along the sandy path barefoot, at one with Lynia.

I found him around the next curve in the path.

He was resting against a tree trunk, eyes closed, with the suspicious sound of snoring coming from his direction.

I crept up soundlessly, sitting a few feet away while I waited for his warrior senses to react.

He didn't move.

"Iri," I whispered, hoping it was enough to trigger something.

Another snore greeted me.

I wiggled his foot and he jumped.

I leaned back in case he woke up swinging. "Sorry, I need to talk to someone."

"I wasn't sleeping." He cleared his throat, stifling a yawn.

"So, you weren't just snoring?" I pointed to the tree where I'd found him.

He ran a hand through his disheveled hair, then stretched. "What is it you want to talk about?"

"I need your opinion on something." I hesitated, wondering if he would tell Beru. I shook my head.

He was loyal, and no matter what else, he wouldn't betray a confidence. "Is this about the priestess?"

"No. Well, sort of." I stuttered, feeling foolish. "There's something I'm having a hard time with and I need advice on how to fix it."

"Beru?" He leaned back against the tree trunk, a knowing smirk on his face.

"Okay. Yes, it's Beru." I let out a sigh at how silly I sounded to myself right now.

"I've noticed you've been off with each other lately."

That was an understatement. I knew if Beru had confided in Iri he wouldn't tell me, but maybe he would offer advice based on what he knew. But I couldn't tell Iri, Beru was the key, because I couldn't risk him slipping accidentally.

I sighed, letting my shoulders relax as I admitted a truth I could share. "I just want things to go back to how they were."

"Let up on him. He's not used to living life like us. He must adapt to living on the outside without his family. It must be lonely." His voice was warm and understanding.

I felt completely insensitive as my cheeks began to burn. I hadn't considered how hard it would be for him. "Does he talk about his family much?"

Iri smiled, a knowing look crossing his face fleetingly. "He misses them."

I knew he wouldn't betray Beru's confidences, but I needed to know one thing. "Does he hate me?"

"He knows how much pressure you've put on yourself. He's forgiving. You need to talk to him about this." He squeezed my shoulder, sharing his strength.

I knew he was right. The simplest advice was always the hardest to follow through on. "How are you feeling?"

"This place is magical. I've never felt younger." He stretched his arms as if fully appreciating his full strength.

"I feel the same. The air, the trees, the water. It's all so relaxing. I hope we can stay for a bit longer." I laid back on the grass, wondering if I should push the subject of Beru any further.

"I'll check in with Captain Rose. I think we could all use some rest. I'll come back when I know more." He stood and shoved his boots on.

"Thanks, Iri." I squinted against the sun, shading my eyes with one hand as I watched him walk away.

He waved as he turned down the path. "Just give him some time. He's coming around. He's got things to figure out on his own, is all."

I closed my eyes as my thoughts turned to Beru's family. It stunned me to realize I was jealous. I felt terrible even without saying the words aloud. How could I be jealous of what he'd lost?

Pushing aside the uncomfortable sensation, I focused on practicalities. Healing Beru so he could remember his role as the key was my priority. There was only one other place to turn. One other person who could help me.

Taking advantage of the small island which seemed immune to the magical blockade on the rest of Bruhier, I snuck off into the woods to use my one chance to dreamwalk.

Lying down on a comfortable patch of grass, I closed my eyes and placed my hands on the sparkling red stone Astor had given me to contact Runa. I'd regained most of my strength since arriving at the temple, and there was so much energy around me here it was almost effortless to slip onto the dream plane.

Runa looked furious as she stood from her bed and grabbed a robe. "I require notice of any dream meetings."

"I don't have time. I'm not able to dreamwalk on most of Bruhier because it's protected against magic. That includes dreamwalking. I took a chance on trying to contact you before we left the temple. I'm sorry for interrupting." It was clear I'd caught her off guard.

"Did you find what you were looking for?" She walked out of the room, into a hallway.

I followed her, even though I was unsure she was the right person to talk to. She was the only one left I could think to ask. "Yes, well, no, I mean…"

"Spit it out." She entered a kitchen and began to make coffee.

It felt odd to be in her personal space. She seemed so accomplished I'd assumed she had servants tending to her every need.

I realized I must have been staring when she cleared her throat. "Sorry. Yes. I found out the key is Beru. The Light Woman told me I have to somehow heal his soul. Once I do, he'll remember he is the key."

Runa appeared shocked.

I wondered if it was because she hadn't figured it out before me, but when she answered, it was with awe. "All this time, and he was right under my nose. What do we do?"

Now she wanted to work as a team? I forced myself not to roll my eyes. "That's why I've come to you. I need your help. I'm not sure how to heal him. He barely even talks to me anymore." I was close to giving up on a relationship of any kind with him.

She stopped pouring her coffee to give me a searing look. "Don't give up now. You've come too far for that. Remember, you've felt close to him in the past. You can get there again."

"I'm not sure he'll forgive me." I leaned against the wall,

remembering how many times I'd pushed him away while trying to deal with my confusion. Now to top it all off, I had heartburn from the guilt of not telling him he was the key.

"Forgive you for what?" She looked mildly curious, but not sympathetic.

"Never mind. Just tell me what to do." I knew it was time to put saving him and closing the prison over my feelings about our relationship.

"You've got to break him. Break him so you can build him back up. That's how you'll get the key."

CHAPTER 24

Before I knew what was happening, I'd slipped from my conversation with Runa and had pulled Beru into the prison with me.

His eyes bugged out when he realized where we were. "What are you doing?"

"I don't know. I fell asleep, and I guess I was unsettled about how things have been between us." It wasn't a lie, but it wasn't the truth either. I suspected Runa had somehow caused this.

"Take us back right now." Beru whirled around, eyes narrowed as he scoped out our surroundings.

"I can't." I held my hand over my ears, fearful of telling him the truth. I wasn't ready to tell him all I knew.

"What do you mean you can't?" He stalked over, grabbing my shoulders as he tried to get me to look him in the eyes.

I wrenched myself away and backed up. I needed space to think. I didn't have a plan. It wasn't supposed to happen this fast. How was I supposed to heal his soul from inside the prison?

Wait. Something must have happened here to make him forget he was the key. "You wouldn't have been able to come back with me unless you're still connected to the prison somehow."

"I'm not connected to anything. I never wanted to see this place again." His entire body had tensed for battle, but I moved closer anyway.

Grabbing him by the hand, I looked up and pleaded with him. I needed him to believe me. "You're connected to the prison. I need to figure out how if we want to keep the walls up."

He stared down at me for a moment then turned his head to look around. I wondered if this meant he was remembering and felt hope rise in my chest.

When he looked back at me, it was with a new calmness. "What do you need me to do?"

"I need you to remember why you're tied to this place, beyond the obvious." I had no idea what I was saying, only that my gut, and Runa, were telling me to push now.

Beru sighed, sitting down on a fallen log, and resting his head on his arms. I waited, letting him think as I watched emotions flash over his face. Maybe he'd be able to remember something I could heal him with.

"There's nothing. I don't know how I'm connected to it. Every night I have nightmares. The idea my family thought the worst of me..." He sat up, not finishing his sentence as his eyes swam with tears.

Instantly, I knew his connection. His family. Or at least his thoughts about disappointing the people he loved most. I didn't have time to figure out anything else, because Beru stood and looked over to the side. Three massive ur'gels were headed our way.

Neither of us had any weapons. We searched the ground and our surroundings for anything we could use to hold them off. I found two long sticks with some girth to them. They'd have to do.

"You take the one on the left, I'll take the one on the right." He said quietly, obviously not wanting them to hear his plan. "Whoever kills first gets the leftovers."

"Well, look who it is. Dag'draath's plaything." The ur'gels laughed unpleasantly, serrated teeth glinting in the light.

We separated slightly so we'd have more room to fight.

They wasted no time, and the smallest of the three launched at me.

I knew size didn't mean anything, holding my stick like a sword and praying I would be quicker.

My opponent laughed and I vowed to use his overconfident attitude to my advantage. He pulled out his sword and swung it cleanly back and forth in a figure eight in front of him, clearly able to disable me at any point.

I dodged his attempts to knock the stick out of my hand as we danced around each other. Every time I retreated, he lunged with his sword. Around and around we went, as I tried to hold my own against a larger opponent with a better weapon.

I glanced at Beru.

He was fighting both of the other ur'gels masterfully, making the stick against sword look a lot more equal than I was. He caught my eye and called out while keeping his eyes on his opponents. "You okay?"

"I'm holding. You?"

"Same." He cracked his stick on one of the ur'gel's wrists, causing him to drop the sword. In one smooth roll, Beru dove. Catching the sword, he rose up beneath the disarmed ur'gel and plunged it into his chest. "One down."

The loss seemed to energize my opponent. He sped up his jabs and landed a solid blow, scraping my arm.

My stick fell from my numbed fingers even as I healed my injury. It tingled and ached but worked. Unfortunately, I was now weaponless.

The ur'gel smiled as he approached, his dark blue-gray skin tight against the sharp teeth, his eyes full of a dark joy.

I crouched, preparing to duck and roll when Beru appeared behind him, ramming his sword into the ur'gel's back.

As it fell to the ground, I grabbed his sword. "Two down." I looked for the third, determined to make him mine now I had an actual weapon.

"He's gone. Likely for reinforcements." Beru sat down, breathing heavily. "How's your arm?"

"I healed it. How are you?" I looked him over for injuries.

"I'm good." He threw his sword down by his feet. "They'll be back soon."

"We need to find a place to hide. You have one?" I looked at him for direction.

"I have many. Let's go."

He stood, and making sure to keep the swords handy, we cautiously approached a nearby building.

"This will do." He forced the door open and we barricaded ourselves inside with a chair. He dusted off a couple more to sit on, pushing a large box into the middle to use as a table.

"Cozy."

"It'll do." He took a seat, looking tired. "They'll be back eventually. We need to get out of here."

"I think I know why you're drawn to the prison."

Beru had taken off one of his shoes and was dumping out the rocks.

I waited, but he didn't reply, so I pressed on.

"Your family is the anchor keeping you here." I waited for backlash.

Instead, he took a deep breath and looked up from the ground. "Go on."

"Your family was the only thing keeping you human. It kept you sane, kept you going. But because of that, it's like some part of you is still stuck here, with them." I reached over and touched his arm, but he flinched and pulled away. I waited for him to speak, but when he hadn't after several long moments, I broke the silence. I knew he wasn't going to like what I thought, but it needed to be said. "We need to break your connection."

"I'll never break the connection to my family. I don't care if I see this prison every time I close my eyes." He stood and began to pace back and forth in the cramped space.

"I'm not asking you to break your connection with your loved ones, just remove the prison from your memories of them." Even as I said it, I knew it didn't make much sense. I needed Runa to help me, but I couldn't talk to her from here.

"All right. So how do we do that?" He stopped in front of me, eyes full of shadows.

I could see his pain in the way he was studying me, like I had all the answers to remove his turmoil, if he could just find them in my eyes. It made me feel competent and like a complete imposter. I knew so little but for his sake, I had to pretend.

I stood up, taking a deep breath as I went for it. "Hold my hands and don't let go."

He lifted his hands flat in front of him and I placed mine on top. "Close your eyes and try to relax."

I closed my eyes after him. I needed to bring him back to that day in the village when his family got attacked. I'd never heard of a dreamwalker going back in time, but I had to try. It was the only thing I could think of to break the connection.

I prayed only the link to the prison would break, not his connection to his family. Or his sanity. I pushed my fears out of my mind, focusing instead on bringing us back to the village where they had lived and worked, relying on his energy and memories to take us there.

Inside the cabin, the fresh wind buffeted my face and the smell of heavily spiced beef tantalized my nostrils. I opened my eyes to see tears streaming down his face.

"How?" His eyes were wide, then he looked beyond my shoulder and his face went completely white. I turned to see what he was looking at as disbelief filled his voice. "It's Melinda."

An attractive blonde held a basket on her arm as she led two boys and a little girl behind her through a busy market.

Beru tried to pull away to follow them, but I grabbed his hands more tightly.

"You can't let go, I'm sorry." My heart stung watching him.

Such a depth of love. It was hard to restrain him, but necessary.

"I have to speak to them again. Please, I have to." Tears spilled out of his eyes.

My eyes stung as I shook my head. I wanted to let him go, but I couldn't. "They can't see us. We can't interact with them. I'm so sorry, I have no control over it."

As he called out to them, I saw him for the first time without his guard up. He was more beautiful than I could have imagined. "Melinda! Thurston, Jahron, Vivi!"

"I'm sorry." I wanted to end it. I couldn't bear to witness his heart shattering all over again.

He turned to me then. "We have to stop the attack."

"There's nothing we can do to stop it. We have to watch it happen."

He turned to me, blinking rapidly and frowning.

I knew he was confused and didn't understand the fact I'd let him watch the attack if he couldn't help, but the fighter within him wouldn't accept my answer.

"Try, Aria." His voice was firm, ordering me to change my mind.

Then we heard the screams.

I had to struggle to hold on to him as his instincts told him to run toward them.

Ur'gels teemed over the small village in numbers they

couldn't have fought off even had he been there. It was clear they were there to destroy Beru's family.

I watched helplessly as Melinda dropped her basket and turned to Thurston and Jahron, wrapping her arms protectively around them even as she searched for Vivi, who was missing from sight.

Ur'gels descended on them. A single arrow pierced her back and she fell to the ground noiselessly. The boys shrieked with fear as they tried to pull her up, crying when she didn't move again.

Beru's silent sobs racked his body and I felt them deep in my soul. His pain was unbearable now he knew how his family died. He had lived on while his wife and children died young. There was no mystery anymore, no reason for his connection.

I held on to him as he turned away from an ur'gel approaching his sons with a sword. I couldn't watch either, so I scanned the crowd for his daughter. Perhaps she'd escaped?

Finally, I saw her.

She ran as fast as she could, but it was no use.

Ur'gels descended on her, taunting her as they shoved her back and forth in the circle they'd formed around her.

I kept him turned away, so he wouldn't have to witness their cruelty as his daughter cried out for her mother.

As her cries halted abruptly with a single knife to her stomach, Beru pulled out of my sheltering arms. Vivi looked in our direction and reached a hand out, mouthing one last word. "Daddy."

She slumped lifelessly to the ground. As she landed, he lost his strength and fell as well, saying her name in a broken voice.

He wept as he let go of my hands, but I followed him down. I had to maintain our link to get us back to the island or we could be stuck forever.

I tapped into his pain, the most powerful form of energy,

and in an instant we were back on the island, in the forest clearing where I'd contacted Runa.

Beru sobbed and clung to me, unaware we'd returned.

I held him back, paralyzed at what I'd witnessed. Had I known what we'd see, I wouldn't have put him through it.

Even for the sake of remembering he was the key.

What had I done to my friend?

I had done the unimaginable. I had broken the unbreakable Beru.

CHAPTER 25

Beru had lapsed into sleep since our return. Priestess Lunla graciously allowed us to remain, designating a small house for our use while I stayed by his side day and night.

I prayed once his hurt subsided, he would come back to us.

"How is he?" Sade entered the room with a pitcher of water, pouring it into the wash pan beside me.

"The same." I forced a tired smile, rubbing my face in a vain attempt to remove some of my fatigue and guilt.

"Have you done any healing sessions today?" She refilled my glass, pushing it into my hand.

"This morning. He's hidden himself very deep in his mind." I took a sip, then placed the glass beside me and dipped the washcloth into the cold water to wipe his face.

"You want a break?" She offered as she sat beside me, patting my leg.

"No. I can't seem to leave his side. I can't let him be alone." I held back tears as the memories of his family being murdered in front of him intruded.

"It's okay to step away. I'll stay here so he won't be alone."

She leaned against my side, taking my hand in hers. "We're all worried about you, as well."

"Well, you should be worried about him," I snapped, snatching my hand away as rage filled me.

"We are worried about him, too. But I know he'll get through this, when he's ready."

No one understood.

They all said they did, but they hadn't done this to him.

I had.

They hadn't seen how much he'd loved his family or watched his heart die as they were cut down in front of him. It was my fault he was unconscious and in pain.

Sade pulled out a wrapped piece of cheese from her pocket. "Here, I saved this for you. They have a crazy breakfast menu here, and I figured you wouldn't want the bird's feet."

I ignored her offering, my attention focused solely on Beru and on wiping down his arms and chest.

"His skin is going to be raw if you keep rubbing him like that." She ate the cheese after I pushed it away again.

I threw the cloth down and stalked to the open door, using the frame to hold me up.

Birds merrily dunked themselves in the birdbath as she got up from the bed. The peaceful ordinariness broke my last wall down, and I began to sob. "I can hear their screams every time it's silent."

She wrapped her arms around me. "I'm so sorry you had to see that," she whispered, rocking me back and forth. "I wish I could take it all away."

We didn't speak for a long while as she held me.

The sun shone brightly into the yard and the birds fluttered playfully in the garden, oblivious to the pain of those inside the house. When I was able to compose myself at last, I pulled away and returned to his side.

If he woke, I wanted to be the first one he saw.

"Captain Rose wants to speak with you. Iri will sit with him, if you'd like."

"I'm not leaving. She can talk to me here." My words were soft but firm as I brushed back his hair.

"You want to tell her that?" She grimaced jokingly.

I ignored her attempt at levity, laying my hands on his forehead and arm I closed my eyes, forcing energy into him. When I finally opened my eyes, he was still asleep. My shoulders crumpled at another failure. I'd try again later, when my energy recovered.

I only realized she wasn't beside me when I heard her discussing me with Iri in the hall outside.

They were concerned about me.

I hadn't left him since our return, and I wasn't looking after myself.

They didn't understand.

I didn't deserve to eat, sleep, or be happy while Beru was trapped in his mind. All of those things could wait until he was back. I could handle his anger or hatred, but not this.

"Aria?" Iri called softly.

I wiped a tear from my cheek. "Yes?"

"May I come in?" He didn't wait for me to respond and stepped into the room quietly.

"Yes, of course." I got up from my place beside Beru to make room.

"Captain Rose is here to speak with you." He sat on the chair next to Beru. "I'll stay here with him. I promise to let you know if anything changes."

I watched as he leaned over Beru.

"I'm here for you whenever you're ready." He patted the blanket covering Beru, then looked at me with concern. "She's got urgent news for you, but he shouldn't hear it."

"Okay." I smoothed down my clothes, uncomfortably aware I hadn't bathed in a while.

When I found her, she was sitting in the garden with Sade. They were laughing as if it was any other day.

I crossed my arms as I watched. I was in no mood to gossip and laugh, and wanted nothing more than to go inside to check on Beru.

"Aria, over here!" Sade waved me over, standing and gesturing to her chair.

"Captain Rose." I sat down, avoiding eye contact.

"It's good to see you. No change in Beru?" She raised an eyebrow, pushing a tray of fruit over to me.

I held a hand up, refusing the food. "No. He's still catatonic." I looked away again, uncomfortable with being near anyone right now.

"I'm afraid I have more bad news." She glanced at Sade, and I knew she'd already shared her news with the others.

"Go ahead."

"We've picked up on some reports about more ur'gels on the loose."

I wasn't surprised. Nothing had happened to stop them. I wasn't sure why she thought telling me would do anything. They weren't my problem now. Beru was.

"If it's on the mainland, why do you care?"

Even as I said it, I knew it was insensitive. Ever since I'd pulled Beru back, I felt cut off.

Runa had tried to dream-meet me several times, but I'd ignored her.

Iri and Sade had even tried to get me to look after myself, and I could *smell* how well that was working.

"Where's the Aria I met when you arrived?" She pulled her chair close to mine, so close our knees touched.

"I don't know what you mean." I backed up, trying to regain my personal space.

"You're hidden deep inside. How can you be there for anyone with so much hatred in your soul?"

I turned on her, my anger spilling over. "You weren't there. You didn't see innocent people murdered. They killed *everyone* because of him."

"You haven't killed? You haven't gone to battle?" She lifted an eyebrow, tilting her head as she waited for me to answer.

"Yes, but…" I halted, unsure how to differentiate between the injustice I'd seen and those I'd killed.

"War happens every day. We need to pick a side and carry on. Right now, innocent people are being attacked by Widow, her spiders, and ur'gels who've escaped from the prison *you* broke." She sat back in her chair, shaking her head sadly. "Forty-five reports of villages decimated because of these monsters. You need to come back to the land of the living. People are counting on you."

I leaned against the table, putting my elbows on it, and rubbed my temples. She was right. I'd abandoned everyone since the attacks. I'd let my feelings for Beru affect my judgment. I wasn't sure how to turn this around, or if I had the strength to even start.

"What should we do?" Sade looked at Captain Rose.

"We have to stop them. Have you discussed how to bring down the walls of the prison?"

"Beru is the key. We needed to break him, and we did it. I did it." I crossed my arms. I wanted to fix the prison so I never had to go back there and I could banish it from my mind.

"When he wakes up, maybe he'll know what to do," Sade cut in.

"And if he doesn't? We still have to stop this killing." Captain Rose pushed, pointing out what I had been trying to avoid.

"Could we pay them off?"

"We'd have to speak with Widow. She's probably figured out you aren't working with her and I doubt she'll be open to it." Sade waved for Iri to join us.

I whirled around. "Who's with Beru?"

"He's sleeping." He walked over and sat down at the last empty chair. "He'll be fine, Aria. We're right here."

I fought the urge to run back to his room.

Iri was right. The chances of him waking while we spoke were slim, if he ever woke up at all.

"We were just discussing the raids happening on the mainland," Sade filled him in.

"Should we leave? We can't let them kill our people. Especially since we know how scared they were when we left." Iri was right.

These were people we knew and helped, knowing Widow would be right behind us.

"I have some contacts. Maybe I can find someone to help with reinforcements," Captain Rose offered.

"That's good. Aria, can you speak with Runa? Get a better idea of how many ur'gels have escaped so far?"

I nodded as he began to organize a plan in response to the attacks. I was happy to see him step up because I knew I was useless right now. I'd agreed to contacting Runa, but I was still avoiding her at all costs right now.

"I'm going to sit with Beru. Just let me know what you want me to do." I got up without waiting for anyone to answer and walked back to the house.

"Hey," Sade called as she jogged to catch up with me. "I'm worried about you."

"I know. I'll kick myself out of this soon. I promise. I just need a little more time."

"We don't have time. We have to fight back before we lose more people. Where is that fighting spirit I know you've got inside of you?" She tapped on my chest.

"She's still here. She'll be back soon." I allowed her to hug me, hoping it would convince her.

She wrapped her arm around my shoulder and spun me to face the view. "He'll come back to us. But until he does, we need a plan. We have to stop the ur'gels, or we'll be screwed if Dag'-draath escapes." She squeezed my shoulder, taking some of the edge off her words.

She was right.

I needed to get back to myself now. I had to be ready to be strong when he came back to us because he would need me. I closed my eyes and soaked in the energy from the land around me. I felt the hard knot of anger begin to loosen, just a little.

We stood overlooking the view above the clouds. It was so peaceful and inviting, for a moment I almost forgot the horror we had been living through. And it was just the beginning. With more ur'gels escaping, it would only be a matter of time before Dag'draath got out. For all we knew, he could be roaming our world right now.

"We won't be able to hide here forever." She shook her head.

"I know. But we need this for now. For Beru. When he's better … I'll figure out what to do next."

"Well, you'd both better hurry up. The world can't wait forever."

Continue reading this series, Legends of the Fallen, with book 3, Soul Healer
https://books2read.com/u/38rjw6

Like the series Facebook page to stay up to date on all new releases
https://www.facebook.com/LegendsoftheFallen

ABOUT THE AUTHOR

J.A. Culican is a *USA Today* Bestselling author of the middle grade fantasy series Keeper of Dragons. Her first novel in the fictional series catapulted a trajectory of titles and awards, including top selling author on the USA Today bestsellers list and Amazon, and a rightfully earned spot as an international best seller. Additional accolades include Best Fantasy Book of 2016, Runner-up in Reality Bites Book Awards, and 1st place for Best Coming of Age Book from the Indie Book Awards.

J.A. Culican holds a master's degree in Special Education from Niagara University, in which she has been teaching special education for over 13 years. She is also the president of the autism awareness non-profit Puzzle Peace United. J.A. Culican resides in southern New Jersey with her husband and four young children.

For more information about J.A. Culican, visit her website at: www.jaculican.com.

ABOUT THE AUTHOR

H. M. Gooden has been scribbling on everything since she first learned how to hold a pencil. While often told that her handwriting was atrocious, she persisted, and upon discovering computers and learning how to type, she realized that she was no longer limited by her (admittedly) messy writing.

Unfortunately, life and work and family have conspired to make it only possible to write in the wee hours or at coffee shops, so most of her love of reading and writing are indulged at times when only vampires and insomniacs abound.

Beginning in October of 2017, her love of writing and the characters in the world she has created burst into public view in her first book, Dream of Darkness, which follows the adventures of a group of girls fighting evil with abilities that H. M. Gooden would love to have.

As a result, 4 am has become even busier trying to find out what will happen to her paranormal buddies in the future, and book six, seven and eight are in the works.

ACKNOWLEDGMENTS

Editor: Frankie Blooding
Cover Artist: Christian Bentulan
Formatting: Dragon Realm Press

www.ingramcontent.com/pod-product-compliance
Lightning Source LLC
Chambersburg PA
CBHW061133200626

46817CB00016B/1318